GUARDED HEARTS

STARLING BAY BOOK 6

SIENNA CARR

Guarded Hearts is a STANDALONE romance in the ***Starling Bay*** series. While you do not need to have read any of the earlier books in this series, it might enhance your reading experience if you do because many of the characters in this book appear in the other Starling Bay books.

Starling Bay Series:

Whirlwind Kisses
Winter's Kiss
Maid for Him
Love Letters
Escape to Starling Bay (Books 1-3)
From Faking to Forever
Winter's Vow
Guarded Hearts
Table for Two
A Bouquet of Charm
Christmas Hope

Newsletter sign up: http://www.siennacarr.com/newsletter

Hailey Ross opened her gold cosmetic mirror and checked to see if her lipstick needed touching up. She turned her head to the left and right, frowned at the sight of newly formed fine lines on the corners of her eyes, and checked to see if the red matte color on her as yet naturally full lips was fine.

She was starving; the few slices of cucumber and lettuce she had had for brunch had done nothing to appease her hunger and her stomach gurgled while Val, her publicist and agent, feasted on eggs Benedict and salmon slathered over with a creamy looking butter-colored Hollandaise sauce.

Inside, she was salivating, as well as slowly dying a little each time Val lifted her fork to her mouth. Hailey looked away, choosing to focus on the potted palm trees dotted around the shimmering blue pool at the Beverly Wilshire Hotel.

"Bruce will go with you," Val announced.

"I don't need a bodyguard. I'm going back to my hometown. Nothing ever happens there." It simply wasn't necessary. She only ever needed bodyguards for large crowds and at events like movie premieres where prestigious jewelers loaned her glitzy and ridiculously expensive pieces of jewelry.

"You're taking Bruce and that's that. No buts." She was about to protest further but she knew that when Val put her foot down, there was usually a good reason for it. Hailey's insides slumped. The timing was lousy. She had her eyes on a few meaty movie roles she had auditioned for. There was also the fact that she didn't relish the idea of returning to Starling Bay, a place she had long ago put behind her.

The release of her latest movie, the third in her successful Monica Martins franchise, had been delayed by six months due to a horrific helicopter crash involving the director and several members of the cast. Luckily, she hadn't been aboard the flight. The director's life had hung in the balance but he was now on the long road to recovery. The movie had finally released and the premiere had taken place in LA last month.

Unfortunately, she now had to attend a second movie premiere in Starling Bay.

To compound matters, one of the TV networks had signed to produce a documentary covering her life story from her years as a gawky teen with humble beginnings in the small town she had grown up into where she was now, a Hollywood A-lister. This also had been delayed. She had been secretly hoping that the TV network would hold off on the documentary, but they seemed as eager as ever for it to go ahead. There was no way out of it. She had to return to her hometown.

She hated the thought of her bodyguard tagging along with her. Bruce would stick out like a sore thumb with his sinister-looking dark suit and shades. She tried once more to appeal to Val. "It's really not necessary for Bruce to tag along."

"You can drop him once you've finished filming the documentary and the premiere is over."

"But it's only in Starling Bay!"

"It's a condition of the studio, Hailey. Please don't keep going on about it."

"What is it?" Hailey asked. Val was holding something back. "Is it the letters? Did they start up again?" In the last few months, she had been receiving letters from one particular fan. These weren't like the types of letters she was used to—friendly and full of admiration. This fan professed his undying love for her and got angry about the villains in her movies. Val had obviously been concerned about it enough to beef up the security at the main events.

"No. They haven't started up again."

"You'd tell me, wouldn't you?"

"Of course I would tell you."

It was normal in her line of work to attract a fair share of weirdos; it was part of the package for being in the public eye, for taking on the sort of acting roles she did where she was eye candy. Curves and long legs. The Monica Martins action movie franchise in which she played a feisty heroine on various quests in remote parts of the world had propelled her to another level of fame. Too bad her outfits consisted of the shortest of shorts and skimpy tops. No man in a similar role, save for Tarzan, would be expected to wear such skimpy clothing in such harsh places and climates. It seemed to be only the women who were expected to wear such things—another reason for her wanting to move away from these cheesy roles and look for something more serious.

Her security detail had been beefed up in recent months and while Val had refused to show her the letters—not that she had particularly wanted to see them—the extra protection wasn't something she welcomed.

"Then there's nothing to worry about."

Val set down her silverware and shifted her shades further along her head. "There's absolutely nothing to worry about, but the studio is going to give me grief if I let you go alone. Just take Bruce, pretend he's invisible and enjoy your visit."

Hailey snorted. Returning to Starling Bay after so many years didn't feel like an enjoyable visit. "I'll be bored sick in no time." Her life back then, as a tall and skinny teen, had been boring in comparison to her life now. She had towered above others at school and had found herself the center of unwanted attention from boys. At the age of thirteen, a TV scout discovered her during his visit to Starling Bay. A photoshoot followed, and then she got a bit part in a TV commercial. Not long after that she was lucky enough to try out for a children's TV show. With her sparkling blue eyes, blonde hair and charming smile, it was enough to get her the role. When the bright lights and glamor of Hollywood had beckoned, she left.

But returning to that same small town was a different matter. Now she was afraid of not fitting in, of causing a commotion, of old memories from a less pleasant time resurfacing.

On the flip side, she was still recovering from the exhausting post-release and publicity schedule, appearing in TV shows in order to promote the movie. In that respect, maybe spending some time in a small town wouldn't be such a bad thing.

"Oh, and you have a signing event at the local mall. I'll deal with the management there and have the appropriate merchandise sent over."

"What merchandise?" Two events to deal with were bad enough, and now Val was adding a third.

"Monica Martins swag, I'll put something together with the marketing department. You just have to look pretty and sign autographs and be nice to your fans."

"I'm always nice to my fans."

Val tapped her finger thoughtfully on the long stem of her glass. "I'm just wondering …"

Hailey braced herself. Val could come up with some hairbrained ideas sometimes. "Wondering about what?"

"Whether we should have Big Rock show up to surprise you."

She clenched her jaw tightly. This was the second time in as many weeks that Val had brought up Big Rock, her friend and a former child star whom she had known from her first TV show. He was quickly climbing the ranks of Hollywood royalty thanks to his huge summer blockbuster hit. The name had stuck because he was a huge guy of Herculean proportion, and he'd been called Rock in the teen show. His real name was Rick Moretti. She was happy for him and his success, especially because it had been long overdue, but she was also aware that the studio liked to put people together in the hopes of driving fans wild with false rumors. "Why?"

"It's good publicity. You guys have been seen out and about."

"We've been catching up. We know one another. We have friends in common."

"You certainly photograph well together," Val remarked.

She balked at the idea. Val had been after her to do more publicity stunts with Rick ever since a photo taken at an awards show—when she had presented him with an award—had gone viral. Because they knew one another, their chemistry that night—both when she kissed him on the cheek to give him the award, and at the after-party later—seemed to have caught a mood. They looked good together; there was no doubt about that. Big Rock was tall, like her, but dark-haired and muscular. He was handsome in a rugged way, with dark brown eyes and an attitude. The media had gone wild. While she could see how they were a celebrity magazine's dream couple, there was no chemistry, not that anyone would have noticed. Surface level was all that counted in Hollywood.

It was never anything deeper, but ever since that night, Val had started suggesting that she and Big Rock do some publicity stunts together, or accidentally show up at the same bar and restaurant where, magically, paparazzi would be waiting.

She had been horrified by the suggestion, and though Val hadn't said it in such direct terms, Hailey was all too aware that a fake romance could help with the buzz of publicity.

Hailey didn't like the idea of that and she did not want any part of this. "No. Please don't bring that up again."

"Okay, fine. But *I* would love to spend a week in Starling Bay," exclaimed Val, sliding her sunglasses onto her face again. "It's *such* a pretty little place." Val had visited Starling Bay when she had a week's vacation time to use up. She had gone with her boyfriend and come back in love with the town.

Hailey folded her arms and stared at the sunshine reflecting off the calm surface of the swimming pool. She couldn't deny that. It was a pretty place, but LA was home. Palm trees and sunshine. Poodles and high heels. Cocktails under glittering night skies. Sometimes, when the pace got to be too much here, she took off to her second home in Santa Monica. Not bad achievements for a twenty-four-year-old. She was super successful and hugely popular, for *now*—while her latest movie was riding high on its new release ratings, but unless her *next* one did well—and the one after that, and the one after that—she would be forgotten in time. She would still be rich, though not as famous, and over time she would definitely be forgotten.

"I've booked you a suite at The Grand Hotel. It's busy and central, but it has the standard of luxury you're used to."

"I don't want busy." She wanted to avoid fans and forget the disadvantages of fame.

"I could rent you one of those delightful houses by the bay, or you could stay in one of the condos at Forest Heights, a luxury development. I think it's too far. Central is best. I'll feel better knowing that you're in the heart of the town center."

"Why don't you come out with me?" Hailey asked.

"Because I'm working on your behalf here."

Hailey sat upright in her chair. "Be sure to let me know the moment you hear back about the schoolteacher audition."

Val sipped from her glass of sparkling water and made a face. Hailey knew it wasn't from the sharp taste of too much fizz. "Monica Martins makes you rich. Getting that schoolteacher's role will confuse your fans."

"Julia Roberts managed it." She had her heart set on the role. It would be so different than the roles she currently had.

"But *Pretty Woman* made her, and Pretty Woman she'll be for life."

"She doesn't care," Hailey protested. "She's made her fortune, and now she can play whatever parts she wants."

"Julia who?" Val cupped a hand to her ear.

Life in Tinseltown could be fickle. Maybe a visit to someplace more laidback was the thing she needed.

CHAPTER 2

"Who's that?" Jax asked.

"Hailey Ross," Patrick sighed longingly at the poster. "Ain't she somethin' else?" Curious to see what had driven his friend to such an inanimate state, Jax peered at the poster, inching his neck closer. It must have only been put up last night because he knew this mall inside out and he would have remembered Hailey Ross, the famous child star. Like everyone else from around these parts, he'd heard about her but this was the first time he'd paid actual interest in her.

"Wasn't she supposed to have come here in the summer?" He was sure he'd seen posters of her months ago, especially in the new movie theater in Starling Bay.

"They delayed the movie. The director nearly died or something, so they pushed the release date out." Patrick rubbed his hands together. "It's worked out well for us, though, huh, given that we happen to be working here. Talk about perfect timing."

Jax read the details on the poster. "It says she has a signing event here." Why was she coming to the mall? This place was about as far from her world as was possible.

"*Why?* Who cares why?" Patrick was unable to take his eyes off the poster. "She is one sweet, sweet thing."

"Sweet?" Jax was forced to stare at the poster again. Ice blue eyes gazed back at him. He flinched. For a moment, it seemed she was really staring at him. He gave a dismissive snort as he took in the actress's long blonde waves which tumbled down her shoulders.

"Look at those lips," Patrick drooled.

Jax was already looking at them. They were indeed pouty, luscious lips. He shuffled uneasily, vaguely remembering the gangly girl from school who had suddenly left to pursue a crazy dream in LA. She had been the talk of the school for a few days, because she hadn't told a soul before she had vanished.

Then, zap!

She had gone.

The entire family, including an older sister, had all upped and left.

"She's mighty pretty, ain't she?" Patrick's hefty jab to his ribs shook him out of his reverie.

"She's not my type." Though he had to agree, she wasn't too bad looking.

Patrick chortled. "She's out of your league, dude."

Jax snorted because that was hogwash and Patrick knew it. One look at this Miss Cheerleader told him she was *definitely* in his league. He had women falling all over him all the time. His slightly long dirty blond hair, often swept back from his face so as to give the impression of being slick and smart, was a winner with the ladies. As was his security guard's uniform. Nowhere was it more evident that women loved a man in uniform than when they approached him and Patrick, and even then, it was to him they turned—with a giggle, usually followed by a toss of their hair— and not to his slightly overweight double-chinned friend. He felt bad for Patrick sometimes because unlike Jax, Patrick longed for attention but women ignored him.

"Hailey Ross?!" A couple of girls gawked at the poster as they walked past, then stopped beside them to read it. "She's got a new movie out," one said to the other. He and Patrick shuffled to the side, but still within listening distance.

"She's making a show about how she got famous," her friend shrilled with giddy fangirl excitement.

Jax placed his hand on Patrick's shoulder. "They're about as excited as you, dude. I'm going back upstairs." He left Patrick still ogling at the poster.

Hailey Ross was returning to Starling Bay.

Woo hoo.

Not.

It wasn't something he was interested in, even though it would give some of the locals something to get excited about. Roxy wasn't going to be thrilled. He had never been able to figure out why his sister couldn't stand the girl.

CHAPTER 3

"Welcome to The Grand Hotel, Miss Ross." A suited man smiled like a grinning Cheshire cat as he shook her hand. "I'm Russell Brady, the manager of this hotel. We are *delighted* to have you here."

"Thank you." She didn't remember this hotel being so grand, but then no one from her family had ever stepped inside it before.

The manager had despatched two attendants to fetch her luggage. She had persuaded Val not to rent a limo for the purpose of picking her up from the airport and taking her around the town. In the end, she had managed to convince Val to get a stately black SUV.

Conscious of who she was, she didn't want to cause any inconvenience to the townspeople, nor did she want any special attention. She had no idea how things were going to be when the film crew showed up to shoot the documentary, though Val had hinted that filming would last for a few hours a day. This was all she had to give up of her time. The plan was to conduct interviews with her in some of her favorite places but once that was over, she had the rest of the day to herself. That was still a few weeks away and she planned to do a little low key sightseeing of her own before then.

"I'll show you to your room, Miss Ross," the manager told her. He seemed eager to ingratiate himself with her, a trait she was well used to by now.

"I can find my own way, thank you." She didn't want or need to put up with idle talk in the elevator.

"If you're sure."

"I'm sure."

She got into the elevator and pressed the button to ascend. Bruce followed her faithfully. He would be staying in the suite next door. The elevator ascended in silence. There was no need for conversation.

In most of the hotels she stayed at, she was given the penthouse or top floor suite. It was always the most prestigious and costly. She was used to glamor, first class and a life of luxury, and she had no idea of what to expect here but upon opening the door to her suite, she was pleasantly surprised. On entering, there was a large living area with two huge couches adjacent to one another. A thin black plasma TV hung from the wall. A coffee table graced the center of the room displaying a beautiful vase of flowers. Behind one of the couches was a medium-sized dining table and chairs, and another vase filled with brightly colored flowers. She walked through and opened the door to her bedroom. It was big, white and pale pink, tastefully decorated, with a shiny, sleek en-suite.

She was impressed.

It was beautiful.

"I've checked everything," Bruce assured her. He had entered first and checked everything.

"You won't have to do that here, Bruce," she said as the porters showed up with their luggage. Hailey tipped them, and they thanked her, their expressions full of delight.

"Your itinerary is blank tomorrow," Bruce stated, hovering around in the doorway.

"I won't be leaving my room. I'll need to get my bearings."

"You know where I am if you change your mind." He gave her a goodbye nod.

She closed the door and breathed out a huge sigh as a wave of nostalgia hit her. The sight of a few places she had seen on her way here had brought back bittersweet memories. Her family hadn't been well-off, but she had been happy at home. School not so much. She recalled walking on the beach with Claire, her best friend who she was still in touch with. They often collected seashells and sometimes bought ice cream from the shop along the beach front. Mostly they used to lie on a picnic blanket on the sand, and giggle and talk as they watched clouds form and took turns in guessing what shapes they made.

She felt strangely happy to be here and looked forward to the prospect of visiting old places so that she could savor life as she had lived it, before she went on to find worldwide fame.

At least she wouldn't have to get up at 4:00 a.m. to drive to the studio. Despite what many thought, the life of an actor wasn't always steeped in glamor. Days at the studio were often long and hard. Fame wasn't all that it was made out to be.

In comparison, Starling Bay suddenly seemed like a safe haven. Her sister had bailed on her, and her parents couldn't cancel their cruise to be with her, so she was here all alone but she could catch up with Claire.

She couldn't think of a better way to pass the time.

CHAPTER 4

"Hurry up and order, Jax."

"Do you talk to all your customers like that?"

"Only the ones related to me," his feisty sister shot back.

"I ordered a lemonade half an hour ago." But Roxy wasn't listening. She had disappeared again into the kitchen. He would probably get better treatment if he were a customer. A paying customer. Because Roxy owned this place, she let him eat for free sometimes. It depended on his finances. His job as a security guard wasn't bad, but it didn't leave much once rent and living costs had been taken out. He usually had a few side hustles going on at any one time—Reed Knight, one of the richest guys in town, usually had enough extra work to keep him busy—and he had also started working at the local mall a few months ago. It was steady income, if boring work and it meant that he could no longer help Roxy out in her diner. She seemed to be working harder than ever, even though she had taken a few people on. His shift times varied and he wasn't starting at the mall until after lunch time today so it seemed like a good time to see his sister.

"Order up," Roxy said, shaking the back of Jax's chair as she walked past again. "I'll be able to have my lunch with you if you don't take all day to figure out what you want to have."

"You've having lunch with me? It must be my lucky day."

He placed his order and soon enough Roxy came over with her plate of food, her face flushed, her manner frenetic. She dove into her jacket potato and wolfed it down. He watched her, as he took a long gulp of his lemonade which had finally arrived.

"What?" Roxy wiped her mouth with a napkin.

"You never stop."

"Never stop what?"

"Running around."

"That's what running a diner is like. Not all of us get to walk around a mall all day."

"What I do is important." He leaned forward, picked up his fork and stabbed it into his plate of pasta. "I keep people safe."

Roxy chortled. "And I keep people fed." She shoveled a few more forkfuls into her mouth.

"Slow down. You're going to choke."

"Can't. I only have ten minutes. Unlike some people." She jerked her chin at him, obviously making a dig at him for sitting around doing nothing.

"I don't start my shift until two today." He worked different shifts. "Hailey Ross is making an appearance at the mall," he announced matter-of-factly, then waited for his sister's response. It came soon enough. Roxy stopped eating, then made a face. Her nostrils flared.

"I know. I saw her last night. She's staying at the hotel."

There was only one hotel fancy enough that someone like Hailey Ross would stay at. He took a sip from his drink. "What were you doing at The Grand Hotel?"

"Never you mind."

"Were you on a date?" A wicked grin crossed his face at this unlikely scenario. Roxy was too busy for romance. She was mostly always at work and she didn't have much of a social life. Her going out was unheard of.

She continued eating and ignored his question which further piqued his interest. "It *was* a date," he deduced, given her reluctance to say anything.

"I was at The Olive Tree with friends."

"You never have time for friends." Ever since she had taken over the diner from their parents, she had worked almost seven days a week and the longest hours. His job as a security guard might be boring, and the most exciting thing might be apprehending some daring kids who'd tried to shoplift, but at least he didn't sell his soul to it. He wasn't married to his work, which, by the looks of it, Roxy sure was.

"Well, I made time last night, and we went out for something to eat, which is how I saw that woman make her grand entrance at the hotel."

"*That woman*?" he mimicked. "Grand entrance, huh?" He could see it now, the actress sweeping in with an entourage, a couple of bodyguards, cameras flashing, and she in her shades and bright red lipstick.

Roxy rolled her eyes. "Miss Glamorpuss walked in with her bodyguard and the manager went running to her side." She shivered in disgust. "That creepy little man."

It wasn't the picture he imagined. "One bodyguard?" Now he was interested. "Was he built? How big was he?"

"I don't know. I didn't pay any attention to him. It was Miss Glamorpuss I was looking at. So were all the other diners."

"What have you got against the woman, Rox? Did you know her as a friend?"

"She's no friend of mine."

"Why don't you like her?"

"She thinks she's special."

This surprised him. "Did you *know* her? Like at school?" He sat forward, wanting to know the details so that he could later relay them to Patrick.

"She was at our school. You're probably too young to remember." He knew she had been at the same school. There was only one high school in Starling Bay. "I really don't remember talking to her or anything. I don't remember her being there, not until after she left, and then *everyone* was talking about her."

Roxy snorted. "She was a couple of years below you, and quite a few years below me. She was a looker; I have to give her that. She turned heads, even back then."

"So, you never spoke to her? Moved in the same friends' circles?"

Roxy shook her head. "The whole school only started talking about her when she left, and we all found out why. She didn't brag about the TV role. She didn't tell anyone. Her whole family just upped and left. I want to know what she's doing back here after all this time."

"She's not here to see you, that's for sure." He chuckled to himself. "She's making an appearance at the mall in a couple of weeks. She's doing some sort of signing event, and she's also taking part in a documentary."

Roxy looked at him with suspicion. "She's going to be at the mall? Don't you go falling for those big blue eyes."

"As if."

"Oh, puh-leese. You seem to know a lot about her," his sister remarked.

"Patrick has the hots for her. He knows all there is to know about her."

"Ugh." His sister stabbed her fork into her food. "Some things never change."

"Look at you, Hales!" Claire gazed at her with adoring eyes. They hugged outside a rundown building and for a moment Hailey wasn't sure she wanted to go inside. The Q from the peeling letters on Quinn's had rubbed out and was barely legible. "You look so good even when you're not wearing any makeup."

Hailey laughed. "I've had a good night's sleep, and I haven't been on set for a few months. I'm relaxed because I also have no more publicity tours." She clapped her hands together. "I can relax." She glanced at the door to the bar. "Is this place safe?" It looked rough on the outside with its peeling paint and tatty windows.

"Yes, it's safe, Hales! Rudy always comes here. He's the one who recommended it. He says 'hi'."

"Say 'hi' to him." Claire's husband was a lovely guy. They walked through the door, following Bruce, and she immediately felt out of place. Claire had moved out of Starling Bay and lived in the next town over, and this sleazy place was close by which was why Hailey had agreed to come here, but on seeing it she now wished she had suggested the Blue Velvet Bar in the hotel.

Inside, Quinn's wasn't much better. Hanging lights were suspended above pool tables which were in one end and music played on the jukebox. In LA, the retro bars had this type of look and feel but it was all plush, fabricated, expensive. This bar was the real deal.

Heads turned and the chattering quieted to a whisper. Claire's excited, "Oooh, they know who you are," behind her was the only sound to be heard.

Bruce found them a table along the wall in an area which was relatively empty. Claire hugged her again before they sat down. It had been years since their last meeting.

They ordered their drinks and raised them for a toast. "To getting together at last," said Claire.

"To you," said Hailey. "To raising a family and being an awesome mom." Hailey clinked her glass with her friend's. Her friend used to send her selfies of her and Rudy but when the babies started being born, it was all about the babies. Nowadays, Claire sent a picture any time one of them did something—like laugh or make a mess eating. Their lives were so different and with three children aged one, three and four, Hailey understood what a treat this night out was for her friend. She took a sip of her orange juice and looked around. Even if anyone had recognized her, they didn't seem to care and this was exactly how she liked it. "Do you come here often?"

Claire made a sad face. "This is the first time I've been here since before Thanksgiving."

Hailey blinked. It was mid-February.

"It's hard to get out much," Claire continued. "I don't want to pay for a babysitter, and I want Rudy to relax when he gets in. The poor man has been hard at work all day."

"You've been hard at work too." Hailey stared at her friend in sympathy. "We'll have to fix that. We'll have to meet up a lot more now that I'm here. Maybe you and the kids could come over to see me at the hotel sometime?"

"That would be awesome!"

They clinked their drinks together again and spent the evening catching up. She kept her drinks soft, while Claire seemed to enjoy her beer. Every so often she would pepper in remarks like "I don't get to go out much, so I'm making the most of it," as if she was justifying it. It almost made Hailey feel sorry for her, and then scolded herself for pitying her friend. At least Claire had something solid; marriage and three lovely children.

She had nice houses, money, expensive clothes and jewelry, a great social life and career, but she didn't consider herself to be in a better place just because she was rich and living in LA.

It had been a slog, cultivating a career with the cutthroat competition for roles. The pressure was relentless. Some of her peers her age were having plastic surgery and doing what they could to achieve the perfect face and body and convincing themselves that they had a better shot at landing a specific movie role. So far, she had resisted this.

"I'm so glad you're here. It will be like the old times." Claire lifted a bottle of beer to her lips. "Don't worry. Rudy said he'll pick me up when we're done here."

"You don't have to explain. You go ahead and let your hair down." Claire was on her third bottle of beer and she kept apologizing and saying how nice it was to have some time to herself. Hailey didn't know a thing about children, but she could imagine that having three young children was more than a full-time job. They had been friends at school and while there had been a small group of them, it was Claire she felt closest to. She hadn't told anyone about the TV contract, or the hasty plans her family had made to enable her to pursue this new life and dream. She had told her friends right at the end, the week before she left with her mom and older sister to relocate to LA. Her father had come later once the family home had been sold.

She hadn't been prepared that some of the girls from her group of friends wouldn't be over-the-moon happy for her.

Claire had been the only one to be giddy with excitement; Hailey had put the reaction of the others down to shock, not jealousy. She had been surprised when one of them contacted her many years later asking for some money, saying that she had fallen on hard times and was broke, and could Hailey lend her some money for now? She hadn't known what to do but, feeling she couldn't ignore her, she had mailed her friend a check. She never heard back from her after that.

It was all so different with Claire who was genuinely happy for her new life. They wrote letters and emails and kept in touch. Claire and her family had come to LA to visit and when Claire got married to her childhood sweetheart, who Hailey vaguely remembered, the newlyweds had passed through LA. She had yet to meet Claire's children but because they were in fairly constant contact, they were up to date with the goings-on in each of their lives.

Claire squinted at Bruce. "Is he going to hang around the whole time?"

Hailey sighed. "I forget he's even here." She dismissed him with a playful wave of her hand. But she was used to him. Bruce couldn't look inconspicuous even if he tried. In his black suit and tie here in this sleazy bar full of guys in flannel shirts and white t-shirts, he was as invisible as an ink blot on a sheet of paper.

"He's pretty hard to miss." Claire took another swig from her bottle.

"I didn't want to bring him, but my agent insisted."

"Do you have him all the time? Doesn't that feel too clingy, having someone watching your every move?"

"Just for now." She had known that here in this sleepy little town, and especially in this dive of a bar Claire had brought her to, a bodyguard was too much. She had tried and failed to convince Val and now she had to tolerate Bruce. It wasn't his fault that he looked so obviously out of place and like an extraneous appendage that she didn't need. She didn't want to stand out in Starling Bay. She wanted all her comings and goings to be low-key. She wanted to be invisible, and while she had managed to blend in, it was Bruce who was bringing all the attention to her.

When she had first arrived here, the black SUV with its tinted windows made heads turn. People stared when she climbed out and she was glad she had traded the limo for it, but it had her wondering if she should have asked for a more modest car.

"He's getting more attention than you," Claire commented.

"That's because I purposely dressed low-key, and he still thinks he's in LA." Hailey pulled down her baseball cap. Earlier today she had managed to sneak out of the hotel without telling Bruce. She had walked around the bay, marveling at all the new stores that had sprung up. It had been a quick, fleeting walk but she had felt like a rebel for leaving unnoticed and without her security.

"Hey, darlin'." A stocky guy wearing an oversized shirt and a silly grin gawked at her. She shifted back in her seat. "Can I buy you a drink?" he asked.

Hailey shook her head. "No, thank you."

"Aw, come on, darlin'. One drink. That's all I'm asking. I only wanna get you a drink. I'm not asking for a kiss."

"No, really. Thank you."

"Hey," Claire stood up slowly and hissed. "Didn't you hear her? She doesn't want your drink."

The man shrugged before sauntering away.

"He's swaying."

"He's drunk," noted Hailey. She felt a little shaken. No one approached her like this in LA. No one came up to her when she was sitting at a bar or in a restaurant. There was an unspoken rule, a kind of etiquette. The fans and the paparazzi hounded her as she arrived and left restaurants and places, but no one had ever come up to her and demanded to buy her a drink. She looked around for Bruce, but he was nowhere in sight.

Claire glanced around the bar. "Where's your guy?"

"Checking out the exits at the back, probably."

Her friend sat back down. "Are you okay?"

She nodded, even though she didn't feel completely fine. It was the newness of her current situation, of being accessible to people in this way, she told herself. It was a little unnerving, too, but the man looked harmless enough. "I'm fine," she said, as if she was convincing herself.

CHAPTER 6

"*W*ell, hit me over the head with a hammer."

Jax ignored his friend and readied himself to hit the ball, positioning his cue and eyeing the target carefully.

"It's her," his friend hissed, nudging him with his arm and making him completely miss his target.

"Hey!" Jax growled, straightening up. "What did you go and do that for?" But Patrick's mouth had fallen open and a hush descended in the bar. Jax stood up slowly. It was then that he caught sight of her.

Hailey Ross was sitting in the far corner, her blonde locks pulled back into a ponytail. She was wearing a baseball cap, and he only saw her side profile. He wondered what she was doing in a place like this.

Patrick nudged him again. "It's—"

"I can see." Patrick was in love, but Jax wanted to get back to the game. More so because he was winning.

"I have to go over." Patrick smoothed down his hair making Jax wonder why he was bothering. It wasn't as if Hailey Ross was going to ask him out on a date. "Don't embarrass yourself," Jax cautioned. He wouldn't put it past his friend to go up to the actress and declare his love for her. "She looks busy." Some guy was talking to her and her friend.

"How am I going to embarrass myself?"

Jax shrugged. "Dunno. What are you planning to ask her?"

"If I can get her autograph. Heck, I might even ask her if I can take a photo of us together." Patrick straightened himself up and stood taller as if he was trying to flatten his rotund bulging belly.

"Why would you want to do that?"

"Why would I *not*?" Patrick was indignant. "She's Hailey Ross, dude, and as far I know, she's still single."

Jax chortled at the sheer audacity of his friend. Patrick didn't hesitate to think that he'd have absolutely zero chance with the woman. Someone like Hailey Ross, he imagined, probably had a hot and wealthy hunk already. "You're really going to do this?"

"I really am." Patrick sprayed breath freshener into his mouth.

"Are you for real?"

"Yeah. She's here, I'm only asking her for an autograph. She can't say no, unless she's nasty, and then I wouldn't want to know her."

"What makes you think she wants to know you?"

"Who wouldn't want to know me? I have a lot to offer. I'm a funny guy."

"You're hilarious."

"Why are you so scared? It's not like I'm asking you to go over and petition her on my behalf."

He wasn't scared. What he wasn't going to do was make a fool of himself like Patrick was. He knew that if he did approach her, a woman like Hailey Ross would probably look at him as if he were beneath her. He wasn't about to give her the satisfaction of that.

They were worlds apart, which was why he'd been shocked that she was here at all. And then he remembered the mall signing event coming up, and what the girls at the mall had said about her doing some sort of documentary. She was staying at The Grand Hotel, so the chances were high that he was probably going to see her around Starling Bay for the next few weeks.

He watched with amusement, his hand resting on the top of the cue as his friend made his way towards the table. The women were alone now.

As a friend, he should have stopped Patrick from making a complete ass of himself, but his friend seemed to be dead set on his plan, so he decided to stand back and watch the show.

Except that Patrick veered off course and instead headed for the men's room. Jax grinned to himself. The guy had chickened out, but Jax saw the drunk return to the table where Hailey and her friend were. The actress didn't look happy. Her body language —all closed off and inching toward the wall, away from the drunken guy—indicated that she felt threatened.

Jax lowered his head, not wanting to get involved. He and Patrick were still in their security uniforms. It wasn't ideal going out wearing them, but Patrick had wanted to relax after a long shift, and a couple of beers on the way home seemed like a good idea.

He turned to the pool table and surveyed the line-up of the balls, but he couldn't resist. He glanced at the actress again, tried to hold back and resist from getting involved as the drunken guy continued hassling the two women. The guy staggered back a few steps, returned to the bar, then walked back to Hailey and her friend with a big glass of beer.

The idiot.

At least Patrick wasn't that bad.

Jax looked in the direction of the restrooms, wondering when Patrick was going to come back. He was missing a great opportunity to be a hero. Then, he heard a shriek before Hailey sprang out of her seat. Her white slacks were drenched in beer, it seemed like. She looked angry, but she also looked afraid. Her friend jumped up too, but the drunken guy didn't leave.

Without a second's hesitation, Jax bounded over. "Hey, pal." He grabbed the guy by the arm. An empty glass lay on its side with the liquid bleeding out all over the table. "I don't think this lady wants your drink."

"Can you leave us alone?" her friend yelled to the guy.

The drunk tottered a few steps away, but Jax held onto him. "I was only trying to be nice."

"Yeah, well, I think it's time you left these ladies alone." Jax noticed that Hailey hadn't said a word. She seemed to freeze up, something he'd seen when people were so scared, they were almost paralyzed. He could not only see her fear in those big blue eyes, but he could also *feel* it.

The drunk lunged forward and grabbed Hailey's arm. She gasped, and Jax's anger soared. "Didn't you hear what I said, dude?" he yelled and yanked the guy away roughly. "She's not interested."

"Screw you." The guy pushed Jax back. The stench of alcohol hit Jax's nostrils.

"No, screw you." Jax pushed him to the side, well out of the way of Hailey's table.

"Who the hell do you think you are?" the man sneered, stabbing Jax in the chest with his short fat finger.

Jax's eyes narrowed. He'd be damned if he was going to take this. He pushed right back, which was the wrong thing to do with a guy so drunk he could barely stand straight, but he was so incensed, he couldn't help himself. A tussle ensued, with fists flying, until the drunk man staggered back, completely knocking over the drinks on another table, and almost landing on top of one of the customers.

The bartender, a guy Jax knew well, rushed over. "Get the hell out, Trip," he growled at the drunk. "You're banned for a month!" And to Jax, "Get him out of here, Jax."

Jax grabbed him by the collar and walked him out of the door. "I better not see you back in here," he snarled before pushing the man out roughly, into the parking lot. As he started to walk back inside, Hailey rushed out. She looked upset, still as fearful, her eyes large and haunted. "Bruce!" she cried, her voice shaky as she looked around outside. Her friend traipsed after her like a loyal puppy.

Who the heck was Bruce? Her boyfriend? Jax couldn't see anyone else in the parking lot, and he eyed the drunk who was now sitting inside his car, his head resting on the steering wheel.

"Who are you looking for?" Jax asked. The actress turned to stare at him, and for a moment he was lost in the blue of her eyes.

"Thank you," she whispered. She was so much softer spoken than he had imagined. He had expected a diva-ish voice. Something more commanding and stronger. Maybe she was badly shaken up. "Thank you for stepping forward."

"No problem. Glad to help." He nodded, then as an afterthought, asked her, "You okay? You seemed pretty shaken up."

"Of course she's shaken," her friend huffed with more attitude than she had a right to. "You would be, too, if you were in her shoes."

"Bruce!" Hailey called, before getting out her cell phone.

"Who are you looking for?" he asked again.

"Her bodyguard," her friend answered.

She had a bodyguard? Where the heck was he? "Some bodyguard," Jax mumbled just as a huge guy in a black suit barreled out of the door with Patrick in tow. So, *this* was him?

"What happened?" The man's voice was thick and deep.

Hailey turned on him. "Where were you?"

"Yeah? Where were you?" her friend chimed in.

"In the restroom, checking out the exit," the bodyguard replied. "I got talking to this guy." He nodded at Patrick.

Jax rubbed his chin. This was typical of Patrick, not only missing the main action but to get in the way.

"What did I miss?" his friend asked.

CHAPTER 7

"So much for you saying you didn't need a guard in Starling Bay," Val had snapped as soon as Hailey told her what had happened.

"We weren't in Starling Bay. We were in a rough bar on the outskirts, somewhere my friend recommended."

"What were you doing there?"

Hailey explained that she had been catching up with her old friend.

Bruce had been fired. Val had been adamant about that, even though Hailey felt bad about it. "What good is he if he can't protect you?" Apparently, he had gone to the back to check out the exit doors but had ended up talking to someone who turned out to be the friend of the security guard who had come to her rescue.

Val called her back the next morning regretting her hasty decision. She told Hailey to stay inside her hotel room for the rest of the day, and then asked for the name of the guy who had come to her rescue. Hailey didn't know, but Claire recognized the security outfit from the mall he worked at.

"Why do you need to know?" she asked Val.

"He did the job. He was there by your side, unlike Bruce."

"You want *him* to be my new security detail? Please, no," she begged.

"I can't let you be there alone. I can either dispatch someone from here, or we can make use of one of the locals. You'd prefer that, wouldn't you?"

Hailey considered the man who had saved her from the drunk. He seemed to be the exact opposite of Bruce. Casually dressed—even in his security guard's outfit—and he didn't look much older than her. She examined the gold strap on her designer watch, a flicker of uncertainty shooting through her. He looked like a regular guy. Only with longish dirty blond hair and twinkling green eyes.

"I'm going to track him down."

"Track him down?" Hailey sank face-down onto a pillow. The incident had shaken her to the core. She had frozen, just like the time she did when a fan, a middle-aged man, had come too close to her when as she walked along the red carpet at an awards ceremony and had grabbed her by the wrist.

"I'll feel better when you have someone."

"But the security guard? Are you sure?" His indifference to who she was struck her. He had seemed more concerned about her safety than he did about asking her for an autograph—which was something his friend had asked for as she and Bruce got ready to leave.

"I am sure. Do you have a better idea?"

Val's insistence niggled her. "Is there something you're not telling me? Did I get more saddo fanmail?" *Saddo fanmail* was her term for the letters she received from men wanting to be her new boyfriend, or from men so deluded that they already believed they were in a relationship with her.

"No. You haven't. You keep asking me and I keep telling you the same thing. You're just all the way over there. I sleep better when I know you're not alone. Stay inside. I'll update you." Val hung up.

Hailey knew what would happen next. Val would track down that guy for sure. Just thinking about him made her heart do a little flip. She had stared at his face a little longer than she should have. She had been thankful for his help, yes, but there was also something to be said about him stepping in to help her. Chivalry was never dead, but a guy rescuing her from the clutches of danger—albeit in the form of a harmless drunk—was romantic. Her alter ego, Monica Martins, would roll her eyes but Hailey felt a flutter each time she thought of it.

Next time she would suggest where she and Claire could meet, and it definitely wouldn't be in a place as sleazy as that bar.

Val had ordered her to stay inside but she had a few days at least until Val tracked the guy down and tried to convince him to work for her. She had plans to revisit old haunts and places she had loved, and she was fired up to do it now, on her own, before she had to do the same with the film crew in tow.

She was determined to make the most of it before Val hired that guy to be her new tail. This was her chance at freedom. To be able to leave and not have a shadow following her every move. She showered quickly and got dressed. Putting her hair into a ponytail and pulling her baseball cap down low over her head, she quickly rushed out of her hotel room, and through the lobby on the ground floor, past the infuriating manager who thankfully had his back turned and was talking to a couple of guests.

Once outside, she breathed in the fresh air and started to walk.

CHAPTER 8

"Some woman from LA wants to talk to you," the supervisor in charge of the mall's security team told Jax.

"Who?" Jax's brows pushed together. He didn't know any woman in LA.

"I don't know. Wouldn't give her name. Said it was important. You're supposed to be on duty right now, not taking personal phone calls."

"I don't know who she is."

"You'd better call her. She said it was important. Take down her number."

Jax scribbled it down in his notebook and continued walking around the mall, keeping a close eye on everyone and everything. He went up the escalator, and saw Patrick coming down in the opposite direction. The altercation last night between the drunk guy and Hailey Ross, and Patrick realizing that he had delayed and distracted the bodyguard causing him not to be there when Hailey had needed him, had resulted in a frosty standoff between the two men. Ross had driven away with her useless bodyguard, and her friend's husband had arrived not long after, leaving the two men outside in the parking lot.

To say that Patrick was annoyed was an understatement. His friend had practically accused him of making a move on his girl. He was joking partly, but he was most definitely pissed that he'd missed out on being the hero and that Jax had stepped in.

They hadn't gone back inside to finish their pool game.

"Wanna grab some lunch?" Jax asked as the two of them sailed past one another. Patrick gave him the mean eye and didn't answer before soon vanishing out of sight.

When he got off the escalator at the top, Jax briefly considered going after his friend and fixing this childish little spat. He had no idea that his friend would be so mad at him; he had obviously underestimated Patrick's crush on Hailey Ross. Sure, he could see why his friend might be in love with her. She had surprised him with her voice and she had been kind of nice. Nothing like the ice-cold maiden he had expected her to be.

But maybe his friend needed more time to cool down. He decided to take his break alone. Also, the mystery female caller was irritating him. Grabbing a burger and fries from the food court, he sat down at one of the tables and called the number his boss had given him.

"Hello?"

"Who is this?" the woman at the other end asked. Her voice was soft and velvety. Polished and smooth. He grew even more puzzled.

"Who're you?" he shot back. "You called my boss and asked to talk to me."

"Is this Jackson Miller?"

"Yeah? Who wants to know?"

"I'm Valerie Goodman, Hailey's agent."

"Hailey Ross?"

The woman at the other end gave a smooth laugh. "Yes. I believe the two of you have already met."

"It was an interesting meeting." He was curious as to why she was calling him now. "What do you want?" he asked, then remembering his manners, "I mean, what are you calling about?"

"To thank you, first and foremost. I am so glad, and Hailey is so lucky, that you were in the bar. It's outrageous that Bruce left her like that."

"Yeah, well, I was there, so …" He scratched the back of his neck, none the wiser as to where this conversation was going.

"I've fired Bruce. He made a monumental mistake, and I was wondering if you might like the job?"

"What job?"

"The one I'm offering you."

It took a few seconds for the words to sink in and even then, he couldn't make heads nor tails of it. "What job is that?"

"To be Hailey's security detail. Her bodyguard. You're a local, I assume, and you're from these parts so you'll blend in more easily."

"Blend in more easily?" He put down his burger.

"Bruce looked like someone out of *Men in Black*." She laughed.

He didn't connect with the humor.

"Hailey isn't eager to have a bodyguard," she continued, "but I would sleep easier if someone kept an eye on her."

Thoughts—like a raucous group of schoolchildren—ran rampant through his head. He'd been offered a job as the bodyguard of Hailey Ross?

He wasn't sure he wanted it.

Roxy would have a conniption fit when he told her.

But then the woman quoted him a daily rate.

"How much?" His eyes almost bugged out of his head. He'd misheard, surely. But the woman repeated the figure. He drew in a sharp breath. He could earn four times what he made as a security guard, even with the extra evening work and weekend work he sometimes took on.

"I can sense that this is a shock to you?"

"Uh." He didn't know what to say.

"Of course, I'll need references, and a video conference with you and Hailey together—"

"Video conference?" He didn't do video conferences. He wouldn't know how to set one up.

"We can do it on our phones. You've got a smartphone, I take it?"

His gut hardened at that. It was almost as if she considered him to be hillbilly. "Yeah, I've got a smartphone. They sell them even out here in the sticks."

"Wonderful. I'll set a call up with Hailey." She laughed. "I suppose I'd better break the news to Hailey. What time works for you?"

He got off his shift at seven. Eight worked. He told her.

"Eight o'clock, it is."

"Why the video call?" he wanted to know.

"Because I need to know what you look like and Hailey needs to be comfortable with you. Besides, I need to know everything about you before I hire you. You're in charge of a high-profile person, and—"

Once again, he felt as if she was talking down to him. "If she's so high profile, why don't you hire a proper bodyguard? Someone who's obviously worthy of your client?"

"I might have to, if your resume falls short."

He sucked in a breath. He didn't like these out-of-town folks too much. Starling Bay had its fair share of visitors with more money than sense, and his senses were already on high alert for signs of any of these people thinking they were better than him.

He was just about to tell her to shove her job offer somewhere when dollar signs cha-chinged in front of him.

This job would pay *big time.* It was an opportunity he couldn't turn down.

"Besides, Hailey wants low-key," the agent said. "She's back in her hometown and she doesn't want to stand out like a sore thumb."

"Too late for that," he mumbled under his breath.

"What was that?"

"Nothing."

"I'll need to do proper checks on you, but if all goes well, I'll call you at eight. Now, can you give me the name and contact details of your current employer?"

CHAPTER 9

She hadn't had a peaceful day like this in a long, long, long time. It had been blissful walking around Starling Bay by herself, left to her own devices, with nothing to do, no agent to harass her, no casting calls, no relentless pursuit of publicity, no negative movie reviews and no social media posts to stress her out. She needed more days like this.

It surprised her how quickly this turnaround in her mood had happened, all within a few days of her arriving in Starling Bay. The town surprised her. She had expected to feel claustrophobic, as if she had outgrown it. She had expected to miss LA, and nights out with her girlfriends, the Hollywood gossip discussed over cocktails.

She didn't miss any of it.

She had bought a bouquet of flowers from a beautiful florist's shop earlier and as soon as she got back to her suite she added them to her existing vases. The explosion of color; bright oranges, and deep purples with rich red and bright yellow germini, interspersed with bright zesty zingy bulby greens brightened up the place some more.

Feeling hot and sweaty, she showered and put on her skimpy

but comfortable loungewear. Then she looked at the room service menu, trying to decide what to order for later this evening. She was still looking through the menu when her phone rang. She picked it up.

"I have a surprise." It was Valerie.

"What kind of surprise?" She sat up, immediately suspicious, and tossed the menu to the side.

"Well, it's a surprise and I also have some news you might not like…"

Her insides tightened. "What won't I like?" She thought of the worst possible thing—the audition for the schoolteacher's role. "I didn't get it…" But, surely, it was too soon for them to decide?

"No! It's nothing to do with the audition," Val assured her.

Hailey relaxed. "Then?"

"Uh … well …"

"Just say it, Val."

It had to be something bad if Val was struggling to get it out.

Val exhaled loud enough for Hailey to get worried. "It's for the good of your career…"

"Just. Say. It."

"Big Rock's summer hit is still holding strong."

That had nothing to do with her. "And?" But she had a sinking feeling in the pit of her stomach all the same.

"And the two of you look good together."

She knew exactly where this was headed. "So?"

"Do I need to spell it out, Hailey?"

She didn't. Hailey knew exactly what she was getting at, but she was going to make her say it, so that maybe Val might have an idea of how the whole idea sounded.

"It could help both of your careers—"

"No."

"Hear me out, Hailey."

"No."

"Look, you're going ahead and looking at movie roles that you stand no chance of getting—"

"Thanks for your confidence in me."

"I'm being serious, Hailey."

"So am I."

"Yes, which is why I indulge you and let you go ahead and audition for these boring roles. But if you're going down that route, you're going to need to bulletproof your career. This latest movie of yours hasn't done anywhere near as well as the second one."

She wasn't worried, but she knew the number crunchers at the studio would be. "It's not my fault it got delayed."

"I'm aware of that."

"Maybe people got fed up with waiting."

"That's one way of looking at it. Or maybe people would have been even more excited and we should have seen a huge rush when it released."

Hailey didn't know because, unlike some of her actor friends, she didn't keep track of daily box office figures. Once a movie was done, it was done, and she already had her eyes on the next one.

"So, maybe a couple of high-profile events with you and—"

"No." No to Big Rock, and whoever else Val and the powers that be might want to thrust upon her. "Please don't bring it up again."

She heard a sharp exhale of breath at the other end. "Okay. Fine. If that's your wish."

"It is." The phone line went silent. "What was the good news?"

"You don't have to be locked up in your hotel room any longer. I've found a new bodyguard for you."

She felt no guilt for flagrantly disobeying Val's orders not to go outside. "The guy from yesterday?"

"That's the one."

Hailey pressed her lips together. She didn't even know his name. "Are you sure about this?"

"You wanted low-key. I've got you low-key. More importantly, he checks out, that's the main thing."

"Checks out?" He was a security guard working in a mall.

"He was with a small security firm before. Nothing exceptional. He's just working for himself but he often moonlights for other security firms. He's also a black belt in Taekwondo."

Hailey's ears pricked up. Something about him being a black belt suddenly appealed.

Val twittered on, "I'm confident he can take care of you. He showed us he could."

"I don't even know him."

"You've met him, Hailey. And besides, you're not supposed to *know* him, he's supposed to be invisible. You're not supposed to be best friends."

They definitely weren't going to be best friends.

"He'll be next door to you, in the suite Bruce had," Val continued breezily, obviously not sensing any of her discomfort. "He'll be by your side twenty-four seven."

Hailey wasn't even sure why she was feeling uneasy about this guy. Something about him made her slightly self-conscious.

"When does he start?"

"Tonight."

Hailey sprung up from the couch in horror. "Tonight?"

"Don't worry. I've arranged for a video call with the three of us at nine."

"When?" Hailey glanced at her watch a she ran her hand through her damp hair.

"At nine. Or was it eight?" Val groaned. "Let me check my planner."

Hailey's insides twisted. She wasn't ready. She wasn't even dressed properly. She had no makeup on either, and she didn't want this man to see her without her makeup.

"It's been an insane day. I should have called and told you earlier, but I was busy checking out Jackson's references."

"Jackson?"

"He likes to be called Jax for short."

"Jax?" She said the word like a question. Jax. Jackson. The name definitely fit.

"The call is now, at eight!" Valerie cried.

"Now?" Hailey drew in a sharp breath. Her hair was wet, and she was wearing a strappy top and lounge pants with no bra. She was in full-on relax mode.

"Yes, sorry … What happened to you at the bar got me in a panic …" Val sounded uncharacteristically flummoxed.

Hailey jumped up and started pacing around the room. "Do we have to talk to him now? Can't we do it later?" This was almost too much to take in. Her plans for a quiet dinner and evening were suddenly disrupted.

"Too late! He's calling me now," Val announced, "I'll accept the call and you should see him on your screen."

"No—wait!" Irritation clawed at her skin at this new bombshell. But it was too late. She glanced at her phone and the screen split into three. Alongside the picture of Val, there was the security guard, a half-smile on his face.

"Jackson, meet Hailey, Hailey, meet your new bodyguard." Val's voice had never grated on her so much. Hailey stood transfixed, glaring at Jackson's face. She opened her mouth to say something but his eyes blazed back at her. He was wearing a baseball cap backwards and what looked like a black leather jacket. He was rocking the biker boy vibe. One thing was certain, this man was the exact opposite of Bruce.

She felt self-conscious, something she never had with Bruce.

Instinctively, she raised a hand to her hair, knowing it probably looked like limp spaghetti stuck to her head. In the three-way screen-shot, she looked semi-naked in her strappy top. Tossing her phone to the couch, she rushed to her bedroom to grab a sweatshirt.

"Hailey?" she heard Val's voice. "Where are you?"

She quickly shoved her head through the opening and pulled her sweatshirt down. Feeling adequately geared up, she picked up her phone and stared into it. "I'm back."

Val's eyebrows pushed together. "So, this is Jackson, and he's starting tomorrow."

She and Jackson exchanged looks and her heart sank. This was a done deal. It was going ahead. "You said tonight," she said to Val.

"You're eager for me to start, huh?" The man was grinning at her as if he found something funny.

"Val said tomorrow."

"He's moving into The Grand Hotel tonight," Val clarified. "But he starts work tomorrow, unless you have plans to go out somewhere tonight."

Hailey tried to put on a brave face even though the idea of losing her freedom so quickly had further dampened her mood. She had been looking forward to exploring the town by herself, to having a few more days alone. This new bodyguard's instant hiring had completely ruined all of her plans.

"You know what?" Val asked, chattering away and oblivious to the strained atmosphere between her and the new guy. "Why don't the two of you to meet tonight and break the ice a little?"

"What? Why?" She had had brief introductions to Bruce and whoever happened to be her security detail for a particular event. This wasn't necessary.

"Is there a problem?" her new bodyguard asked. His voice was deep and throaty. Funny how that hadn't registered yesterday.

She opened her mouth but didn't know how to politely tell him she didn't want him around. Yesterday's event made that wish obsolete now.

She tried another avenue, hoping to appeal to Val. "Why can't we start next week? I'll be good and stay in my hotel the entire time. I have a lot of new scripts I want to read through and he can start when the film crew arrives."

"He has a name. It's Jax," the bodyguard said.

"Jackson," she said, forcing a smile.

"Uh … Val …, it sounds like the diva doesn't want me around."

Hailey glared at the guy. "The diva?" *The diva?* She was anything but that.

Val exhaled loudly. "I'm sensing some negativity here. What's the problem, Hailey?"

She saw Jackson's eyebrow lift, saw the start of a smirk in the corners of his lips. It only made her madder. She didn't want him. He was too young. Had too much attitude. She was used to older, boring men. Men who didn't press her buttons. This man was pressing *all* of her buttons. She didn't have the mental headspace for his inane jokes and banter.

"Jax," Val turned to him. "You're moving into the hotel soon. Why don't you knock on Hailey's door and introduce your—"

"No," she cried. *No. No. No.* That would be way too awkward. "We'll meet in the bar downstairs."

"You want to meet me in a bar?" he asked.

"I think that's a wonderful idea," Val gushed. "When can you check in, Jax?"

"In the next hour."

In the next hour. Hailey's spirits sank like a stone to the bottom of the sea.

"What time did you want to meet up?" he asked her, and when she didn't say anything, "How about nine?" he suggested. "That should give you enough time to get ready." He flashed her a cheesy smile which she didn't appreciate.

She hung up and wondered what she was supposed to do and say to this new stranger who was charged with guarding her life for the next few weeks.

CHAPTER 10

*H*is world had changed in the space of twenty-four hours. Yesterday he'd been at a bar with Patrick playing pool and having a couple of beers, and today he was meeting a Hollywood actress in the Blue Velvet Bar—as her bodyguard.

Her bodyguard.

Yesterday had taught him that unexpected things could be right around the corner.

None of this seemed real. Not this job. Not Hailey Ross. This was stuff of fantasy. It was what they made movies about, and yet this was real and it was happening to him.

He hadn't said anything to his supervisor at the mall, or to Patrick; he had clocked off his shift early making up an excuse about having an upset stomach, but he'd have to tell them tonight, or at least before tomorrow's morning shift when he obviously wasn't going to show up.

The timeline was tight, but he wanted to see what a one-to-one meeting with the diva would be like. If she was full of airs and graces, he wasn't sure he'd be able to put up with her.

Still, he couldn't wait to see the look on Roxy's face when he told her about the surprising new opportunity which had come out of nowhere.

He quickly packed his things into a small bag, unsure of what to wear, or what was required of him. There was also the problem that he couldn't take too much with him on his motorbike.

Val had said Hailey had a car and a chauffeur—what a life of luxury this woman lived—and that she had a daily itinerary which she would give him to let him know of her movements. According to Val, Hailey hadn't been so keen to come back to her hometown and couldn't wait to get back to LA. She had a couple of events here—which he was already aware of long before Val had told him, but the main reason she was here was to movie a documentary.

At least he had some background on the diva, otherwise he was pretty much in the dark about a lot of things.

Arriving at The Grand Hotel, a place he had only ever walked past, he was thrilled to discover that he had one of the big fancy rooms at the top. He never came here. There had never been any need to. He preferred places like Quinn's and he found it amusing that the actress had referred to one of his favorite bars as a rough place.

As he walked into his room, he almost choked in surprise. It wasn't a just a room, it was almost an apartment, and it was *huge*. He'd been expecting just a bed in a medium-sized bedroom with an en-suite but this place blew his mind. Dropping his bag to the floor he stared, open-mouthed at the huge sofas, the kick-ass TV screen hanging from the wall, the dining table, and coffee table. Walking into the room which would be his bedroom for a short while, he couldn't stop smiling. He was about to pull out his cell phone and call Patrick to show him, but that might cause further friction between the two of them. Besides, he had yet to explain to his friend about his hasty departure.

He opened his bag, pulled out a fresh t-shirt, and ran his hands through his hair. As he was about to leave, he remembered something. Rifling through his luggage, he pulled out his bottle of aftershave and put some on.

This ought to be good enough for Hailey Ross.

He got downstairs and walked towards the bar. Everything about this hotel was fancy and he felt slightly uncomfortable, slightly out of place. He looked inside the bar trying to get a feel for the clientele and now wondered if he was underdressed in his distressed jeans and a black t-shirt. Most of the people in here wore business suits or smart casual clothing.

A server approached him. "Can I help you, sir?"

"Uh … I'm waiting for someone."

"Would you like to wait at a table?"

Not really but … "Sure." It seemed the sensible thing to do.

"Would you like to order a drink while you wait?"

"Uh." He imagined the drinks here were extortionate. He didn't want to pay double or more for something he could get at a reasonable price elsewhere. "I'll just wait, thanks."

He sat at a table away from the door, in a less crowded area, figuring that Hailey would much prefer this to somewhere less private. He looked around the bar, then at the entrance for any sign of her. And then he waited, alternating between glancing at the drink menu and his cell phone.

When ten minutes passed, he grew restless. When another ten minutes passed, he started to get annoyed, and when the next ten minutes after that passed, he was close to getting up and leaving.

He'd come all the way across town to get here on time and not only was she upstairs in the same building, but she was making him wait. She couldn't haul her butt downstairs on time. He had no time for such behavior.

When the server came over to him for the second time that evening, he glanced at his watch, his anger simmering just beneath his skin.

The woman was so blatantly late, he was beyond irritated, but not completely surprised. This was exactly the type of behavior he expected from someone like her.

"Can I get you anything, sir?" a different server asked him.

"I think I'll give this a pass," he replied, growing increasingly sick of giving answers. He rose to leave when Hailey Ross suddenly appeared beside the server. She looked flushed and out of breath.

"Sorry I'm late. I didn't realize you were sitting all the way back here."

"You're late because I'm sitting all the way back here?" he growled.

The server looked at her, and then at him. "I'll let you settle in and then I'll be over in a moment, ma'am."

"That's not what I meant." Hailey sat down.

He clenched his fists, tried to tamp down the anger. "I was about to leave."

She was wearing an oversized sweatshirt and jeans, and her hair was loose this time, spilling out from under her baseball cap. The baseball caps were the only thing they had in common.

"I'm really sorry—"

"You're almost forty minutes late. You only had to come downstairs."

She raised her eyebrow and gave him a how-dare-you-talk-to-me-like-that look. It was warranted. He didn't bow down to people because of who they were, but his anger was disproportionate to her crime. If anything, his anger came from him feeling out of place in a bar like this, and Hailey wasn't to blame for that. "I'm sorry," he said, trying to calm down. "I didn't mean to get angry. I just felt like an idiot waiting here so long."

She looked surprised. For a moment he thought she was going to ask him why, but instead she said, "I should have called and let you know, but I was on the phone. My mom called. I should have hung up. I mean, I wouldn't, I couldn't, her being my mom, you know how these things are."

He smiled, but it was mainly out of relief. She was a completely different person face to face. On the phone, she had seemed not as friendly, but then again, she was an actress. Maybe she was putting on an act now. He sat back down, and all of his hardness melted. She had been talking to her mom, not spending a long time getting ready, or doing it on purpose to make him wait, both of which had been possible explanations he had cooked up in his mind while waiting.

When it came to ordering drinks, he was about to order tap water, but felt suddenly conscious of his status, felt broke and poor in comparison, and hated himself for it—for he wasn't either of those things, but being with this woman made him feel that way.

He ordered a coke, and she ordered tomato juice. Again, surprising him with her choice. He'd expected cocktails or a fancy wine. Champagne even.

He wasn't sure what to make of it. On the three way call earlier Hailey hadn't seemed all that happy about him being her new bodyguard but she seemed miles friendlier now.

"So," he tapped his fingers on the table.

"So," she lifted her glass to her lips. "This feels weird."

"Tell me about it." He looked around, not that any of his friends ever came to places like this, but Roxy sometimes did, and he prayed tonight was not that night. His sister needed some warning before he told her about this new and sudden change in his life.

"You didn't seem so happy for me to get this job."

"Val sprung it on me."

"She sprung it on me, too."

"I don't want a bodyguard," she protested.

"Sounds like it's not your call."

"I don't need a bodyguard, not somewhere like here."

"Didn't seem that way last night." What would she have done if he hadn't stepped in? "You were lucky I was there." He cracked a smile, wanting to break the ice more than to toot his own horn.

Her lips flattened together, as if she didn't like him reminding her. "Is that a line you say to most women?"

Her angry eyes bore into him. Hell. She thought he was coming onto her. "Most women?" He cocked his head as if debating the question. "Definitely not someone like you because you are *so* not my type."

She choked on her drink, and he didn't blame her. The conversation had quickly turned a corner. He hadn't expected it to go this way. Not so soon. Not with someone like her. Not at all.

"Your type?" Her brows furrowed together. She blinked, exaggerating the motion to express her extreme surprise. "You do know who I am, don't you?"

He hung his head in disbelief, saw this as something to tell Roxy about when he next saw her. "A diva," he lifted his head. "Was I right the first time?" Even as he said it, he knew it was wrong. He'd been employed to take care of her, to guard her from harm, and here he was throwing nothing but insults her way. He usually had more restraint when it came to women, even the ones whose attention he didn't want. Hailey wasn't one of those women. Someone like her wouldn't seek his attention but there was something fundamentally wrong in their chemistry.

They couldn't stand one another.

And therefore, this wasn't going to work.

She shook her head and pushed her barely touched drink away. "I'm not in the mood for this. I don't know what Val was thinking hiring you, but ..." Her mouth twisted as if she couldn't find the right words to spit out at him.

Sensing her distress, he suddenly sobered. This had gone wrong and fast, and he could see those dollar signs of income—

the ones which had persuaded him to take on this role and at such short notice—slip away from his grasp. "Shall we start again?"

Her face was set hard. "I'm not sure it would help. This feels odd, sitting here having a drink with you."

"I wasn't the one who suggested it. It was your agent."

She looked incensed. "I'm not used to having insults hurled my way."

He flexed the muscles along his jaw. They had rubbed each other the wrong way. Part of it was his fault. He had a feeling that people looked at him a certain way and made judgments, and he was sure she had, too. They both had. He wasn't completely blameless in all this because he had certain preconceived ideas about her. Now would be a good time for him to apologize. He was just about to say something when she stood up. "We've met. Mission accomplished. Goodnight."

He watched her leave, and then realized he had to go with her. He was supposed to guard her. He rushed out, then realized he hadn't paid. He slipped the server a note and ran to catch the elevator just before the doors closed.

CHAPTER 11

*Y*ou do know who I am, don't you? Where had that nauseating line come from? Hailey collapsed onto the bed and stared up at the ceiling. The meeting had gone horrendously wrong and she squirmed in embarrassment.

What must Jackson have thought?

She knew what he thought because of the disgusted look he gave her. The man had the capacity to bring out her defensive side. He was a player, a biker boy, a Romeo. Someone who clearly thought he was a looker. For him to say that she wasn't his type was outrageous. Not that she wasn't his type, but that he had taken the conversation there in the first place.

She had fired back, but her words must have sounded *so* big-headed. She cringed with embarrassment just thinking about it. This meeting, this exchange, this back and forth with Jackson, it would never have happened with Bruce. As much as she had hated having him, she now wished he was her bodyguard instead of this new guy.

She groaned and sat up, hugging the pillow to her chest because she needed some sort of comfort. This behavior of hers was reactive, and she wasn't a reactive person. She was calm and collected, most of the time. The problem was that Jackson made her react in a way that she wasn't comfortable with.

It wasn't his fault. She had felt a little odd ever since she had returned to Starling Bay, like a fish out of water. It was a strange combination of bittersweet memories from the past mingling with events not going as smoothly as she had expected. The incident at Quinn's and now this introduction with Jackson.

She lay back on her bed, clasping her hands over the pillow which she held like a teddy bear.

She actually liked being back. The sense of peace and quiet, without Val chasing her, telling her she needed to attend an event or be seen at this party, or that she needed to have a fitting for this dress—she liked not having to think about any of these things. It had only been a few days but with no lines to learn by rote, no hopes to keep afloat—aside from that schoolteacher's role she had her heart set on—time seemed to have come to a halt, or slowed down a lot. It grounded her, though Jackson was going to ruin that sense of peace for her. Now he would shadow her, clinging to her side like an unwanted leech.

Sitting at the bar with him dressed like that, distressed jeans and a black tee, with his baseball cap on backwards, her heart had missed a beat when she had seen him. It was the realization that she also wore a baseball cap, that they were the only two who seemed to in that place where most were in formal attire. That first sight of him, before the split-second realization of who he was—caused her heart to jolt.

She wondered if he was always going to dress like that because she much preferred it to the heavy-handed black suit look that Bruce favored. Thinking about it, she wasn't even sure if Jackson owned a suit.

The conversation had been ruined and he'd raced to get into the elevator. The uncomfortable silence inside had been as thorny as barbed wire. They hadn't discussed how this would work.

Bruce knew the drill. He would have an itinerary of her day and would be ready for whatever she had planned.

Jackson didn't know anything, and she knew nothing about him except that he was in the room next door. How would that work? Wouldn't his family or his girlfriend find that odd? Did he even have a girlfriend?

She tossed the pillow to the side. It was pointless to waste her time wondering if he had a girlfriend. It was no business of hers.

Tomorrow she had plans to visit a few places, including the movie theater because she had heard it had been renovated. It was also where her movie premiere would be.

She shuffled up the bed and picked up the hotel phone to call next door and tell Jackson about her plans to leave by 10:00 a.m. tomorrow, but she thought better of it and texted him instead.

Hailey: Be ready by 10:00 a.m. tomorrow.

Jackson: Sure thing.

The next morning when she left her hotel room, Jackson was waiting outside. The shock of seeing him made her stumble back a few steps, as did his appearance. He was wearing nice slacks, a shirt and a tie and he looked as if he was going for an interview. She tried not to make her shock so obvious, but it was too late. He'd noticed.

"What's wrong?" He fiddled stiffly with his tie as if it was an unwanted part of him.

"Uh … nothing."

"You don't like it." He shoved his hands in his pocket. "'Because I'd rather not be wearing this stuff either."

"Don't you have a suit?" It came out the wrong way, sounded patronizing, and it wasn't at all how she meant it.

His face hardened as he tried to rein in a snarl. "Yeah, I've got a suit. I thought you wouldn't want me to wear one. Val says you didn't want your security people to stick out like a sore thumb."

He had paid attention and, more importantly, had acted accordingly. She felt bad for her harsh tone and was about to apologize when he retorted, "I'll wear a suit if that makes you feel better."

"Can't you wear your normal clothes? What you had on yesterday? You'll blend in better."

"Blend in?"

"I don't want to attract attention."

"Should have thought of that when you decided to come back here."

His words prickled her, especially after the way last night had ended. Perhaps this was going to be the nature of their relationship. Instead of having someone who was invisible, who she forgot was around most of the time, Jackson was going to be a thorn in her side.

They stared at one another for a long, uncomfortable moment which stretched out like a length of barbed wire. In the next instant, he disappeared into his hotel room and left her standing in the hallway all alone.

Some bodyguard. She was about to protest when he suddenly appeared, dressed in the clothes he'd worn last night, only he wore a white tee with a flannel shirt over it.

"That was quick," she gasped, because it was so unbelievably fast.

"I can strip off really fast when duty calls." His cool gaze, leveled with hers, making her catch her breath. She wanted to say something back, something short and witty, which would slap him down, but words failed her.

"Sorry about that," he said matter-of-factly. "I shouldn't have left you standing here alone. Some bodyguard." He laughed at his own joke, even as she found it freaky that they both had thought the same thing. "The car's waiting," he informed her.

Remembering to swallow, because her mouth was suddenly parched, she headed towards the elevator.

"Where are you going today?" He pressed the button to go down. "Apparently, you're supposed to tell me."

She ground down on her teeth. It was bad enough that today was going to be so different compared to yesterday. Gone was her feeling of freedom, of being able to roam the town alone. Worse, she was paired up with this annoying man. She heaved a sigh at the effort of having make conversation. This was way too much conversation to be having, especially with her bodyguard. "It's all changed. I have to get used to this new setup, just like you."

CHAPTER 12

She belittled him. Worse, she was patronizing.

The air was charged with unease as they drove in the SUV. He sat in the front with the driver who, thankfully, seemed like a normal guy. He and Jax exchanged short greetings because Val had warned him that there was to be no chit-chat. He understood. This wasn't a date. It wasn't even a picnic in the park. This was a job, and Hailey was the bratty VIP. He had to be vigilant and observant and be alert for any signs of trouble before it found her.

That was funny, because trouble didn't come to Starling Bay. It wasn't that type of town.

Even Quinn's wasn't a bad place. What had happened that other night with Hailey had been a one-time thing. It wasn't fair to tarnish the place just because Hailey Ross had decided to pay a visit and an overzealous fan had stepped out of line. She had been scared, though. He hadn't been able to forget how scared she had looked.

Patrick was still pissed with him. Jax had called him last night, after that train wreck of an evening with Hailey, and told him about his new job. His friend hadn't believed him at first, and

Jax wasn't sure he believed him now either. He would have to find a way to make it up to him and the only thing he could think of that might do it was if he found a way to introduce him to the actress.

That would do it.

He looked out of the window and took in a breath of fresh air. Lady Luck had favored him. Had it not been for that serendipitous moment where he'd saved Hailey, he would most certainly have been walking around the mall right now.

This woman led a gilded life up there in her ivory tower. He balked as he remembered the way she had snapped at him and asked whether he owned a suit. Venturing a glance at the rearview mirror, he caught her looking at him. She looked away quickly, and he suppressed a grin. This was the second time already that she had done this.

He had this effect on women. His bad boy reputation preceded him, though Hailey wouldn't know anything about that. Women fell for his tousled hair, his muscular build, and the black belt helped.

"Where are we going?" He glanced over his shoulder because he still had no idea, and he hadn't heard what she'd said to the driver.

"Miss Ross wants to see Glassmere," the driver answered, when Hailey didn't.

"Yeah?" Annoyed that she hadn't told him, he ignored Val's instruction to not engage in conversation. "What's in Glassmere?" He knew these parts, only because he often did some extra side work for Reed Knight, and Reed usually asked him to keep an eye on his property when he was away.

Hailey didn't answer him or look his way. Instead, she kept her gaze firmly out of the window, which gave him an easy opportunity to admire her side profile. She had a fine nose and full lips, and try as he would, he couldn't easily look away.

"Did I do something to upset you? Or should I report back to Val and say you're keeping me in the dark about things?"

"You're threatening me? Really?" Her eyebrows rose. Then, to the driver, "Anywhere along here will do. If you park up somewhere on the right." The driver obeyed. Jax turned back around to see what Hailey was going to do next. She had rolled down the window, her golden hair down, her eyes sparkling, her lashes long and curled upwards. This woman didn't leave the house without her lipstick and face armor, which was a shame because she was so darn beautiful. She turned to him, her cool blue eyes catching him. "You keep staring at me."

"You keep staring back at me."

"That's because you were staring at me," she tossed back. The driver coughed lightly, making them both stop. Jax faced the front and let out an exasperated sigh. Every conversation they had descended into barbs. This one now was like two four-year-olds having a spat in the playground.

He got out of the car, crossing over to her side before opening the door.

"What are you doing?" she asked, her hand on the handle, getting ready to get out.

"What does it look like?"

She seemed affronted by his tone. He was aware that he shouldn't talk to her like this, in such a brusque manner. She was Hailey Ross, and as much as she annoyed him, he had to respect who she was. "I'm holding the door open for you," he said, adopting a softer tone.

"I'm not royalty. You don't have to do that."

"I didn't know. It's not like you've given me the A-to-Z of this job."

"Val said you'd done security work before."

"I've guarded buildings, not bodies." Perhaps that was too harsh. He let go of the handle.

"You don't have to open the door for me. Only if we're at a movie premiere." She pulled her loose hair into a ponytail then climbed out. Her long, rangy frame seeming even thinner and taller as she straightened up. She was still a few inches shorter than him and standing so close to her out here in the open, the tension of this morning slipped away as a surge of adrenaline coursed through him.

"You have one coming up, Val said." He shoved his hands into the pockets of his jeans. "I need to know the date."

"It's next month. It depends on whether or not you'll be able to stick this job."

There she went again, being condescending, but she must have realized because she apologized right away. "I'm sorry. I don't know why I did that."

"Behaved so rudely, you mean?"

Her eyes widened, and he held back a smirk. He bet she hadn't been spoken to like that before.

"Your personality seems to be rubbing off on me," she retorted and walked away before he could get his punchline in. It was just as well, because they were going to get into another disagreement soon enough. This was nothing like the position that Val had described to him. But most of that had been his fault. Instead of being invisible, he'd done the opposite.

Was it any wonder they were starting to get on each other's nerves? At this rate it wouldn't surprise him if Val sent someone over from LA to replace him.

He followed her as she walked around. This part of Starling Bay was full of sprawling multi-million-dollar mansions set way back from the street and overlooking the ocean. They had long winding driveways, landscaped gardens, and big, shiny and beautiful cars that cost as much as most people's houses, if not more.

It was the exclusive part of town, where rich people lived;

people like Reed Knight. It wasn't for people like him. It didn't surprise him that Hailey hailed from around here and it was another reminder of just how different they were.

"You don't have to follow me so closely," she mumbled without turning around.

"Noted." She was still sore about last night. "This is new to me. Give me a break." He had meant to keep to one-word replies but couldn't resist.

She turned around again, looking surprised. He'd have to curb the way he spoke to her because she clearly didn't like it, and he had to admit, he was plain rude. He couldn't help himself. He should have known better than to think he could work under someone like her. He braced himself for her reply. It looked as if she was thinking of a suitable retort, something sharp and hard to throw at him—like a literary javelin, but she stopped herself.

He stayed back and watched her walk, peering at houses before standing outside one. He assumed this was her childhood home. He returned to the car and leaned against it.

"Not a bad place to grow up in, huh?" he joked with the driver.

"Not a bad place at all."

Jax stared at the house Hailey seemed preoccupied with. Hers was no rags-to-riches story. This diva had already come from money before she'd moved on to Hollywood royalty.

Bored, he whipped out his cell phone and saw a handful of texts from Patrick who wanted to know how his day was going and did he have any photos of Hailey?

'No,' he texted back, before slipping his phone away in his pocket.

It wasn't professional for him to be standing around texting when he needed to be vigilant. Unfortunately, this type of work was boring. At least in the mall he had Patrick for company. They would meet up every half an hour or so while they patrolled different parts of the mall, and there was always the hustle and bustle of the busy shopping place with customers scurrying everywhere, like ants across the many floors.

Fed up of waiting, he breathed in deeply, watching Hailey. She was a stunning woman and he wondered what her boyfriend was like. If she had one, he would probably show up at the movie premiere. Now *that* would make for an interesting evening. He was looking forward to it, if only to prove her wrong and still be in her employment.

He forced himself to wait patiently, and when she started to walk back, his hand flew to the car door which he was about to open before he remembered. He also had to hold himself back from making conversation because he wasn't used to this, not talking, not commenting, not being seen. It would take a while.

The driver spoke up. "Where to next, Miss Ross?"

"Back to the town center, please."

They had been driving for a short while when she announced that she was hungry.

"I know of a good place to get some lunch."

"Let's go there then." Her easy acceptance surprised him.

"To Roxy's Diner," he instructed the driver. He hadn't been able to get a hold of his sister last night and this news wasn't the type he wanted to leave as a message. Walking into his sister's diner with Hailey Ross in tow was the way to announce it.

He couldn't imagine the look on Roxy's face.

He was prepared for another gloomy, silent car ride back when Hailey spoke first. "This place has changed, but it also hasn't," she announced. He wasn't sure, given Hailey's changeable mood, and Val's directive, if he was supposed to answer. It would look rude if he didn't. "Changed how?"

"There weren't so many houses here before. They were more spread out."

"Nice place to grow up in."

"I didn't grow up there."

"You didn't?" Then why the heck had she wandered around the area?

"My dad used to talk about it. We would sometimes drive by and he would say one day, one day we might end up here."

He had it all wrong about her. "Yeah?"

"One day, and that day never came." Her voice was dreamy, faraway. A glance in the rearview mirror showed that she was staring out of the window again, her expression softer. "Where are we going?"

"To a small diner. It's nice and cozy and has great food."

"What's it called?" She was suddenly very chatty.

"Roxy's Diner."

"Roxy's Diner? I don't recall the name."

"It used to be called The Diner." When it had belonged to his parents, before Roxy had shown an interest in wanting to take it over. "If we go now, while it's quiet, we can get there before the rush. Assuming you want to eat in."

"I want to eat in. I feel as if I'm on vacation and I want to make the most of it." For once they seemed to be having a decent conversation. No digs, no jibes. If it continued like this, his time with Hailey Ross wouldn't be the headache he was starting to think it might be.

As the car approached the town center, a smile curled on his lips. Roxy was going to get one heck of a surprise.

And she did.

Her face dropped as soon as he walked in wearing his casual clothes instead of his security outfit. But when Hailey Ross stepped into the diner behind him, his sister's eyes seemed to almost pop right out of their sockets.

A server greeted Hailey. Jax stepped in and asked for a part of the diner that was less busy. While Hailey was getting seated, he walked up to his sister who seemed to have frozen in place.

"What's going on?" Roxy's eyes narrowed as she tried hard not to stare in Hailey's direction. A ripple of laughter from a nearby table provided the right amount of background noise. "I have a new job."

Roxy raised an eyebrow. "With *her?*"

"You know who she is, don't you?" He was just checking to see, but he also enjoyed irritating her.

"Of course I know who she is," Roxy snapped.

"Well, I'm her new bodyguard." He took great delight in seeing Roxy's face change expressions from surprise to quiet annoyance.

"You are?" she hissed under her breath.

"She's my lucky break," he answered with a smug grin. The aroma of warm food rolled over him and he was suddenly ravenously hungry.

"What? How?" Roxy, for once, seemed short on words. "And how come you tell me now?" She pulled him and sat him down at a table near the front. He turned to see that Hailey was still in his line of sight. She was, and she was busy looking at the menu. He was unsure of what a bodyguard's lunchtime etiquette was; whether he should sit near her, with her or far away while she ate.

"Hey," Roxy slapped his arm lightly, getting his attention. "How?"

He told her the whole story, about how he'd been at the bar and stepped in when a drunk approached her and how he had received the strange phone call from her agent the day after. By the time he was finished, Roxy was sitting back in her chair, her arms folded defensively. "I can't believe it."

"Me neither." He gave her a huge grin. Now that he'd been out for the day with Hailey, he saw that this was going to be an easy job. Being chauffeured around and just keeping an eye on her, was simple, and when they weren't bickering, it wasn't so bad at all.

"Why don't you go over and say 'hi', you being the owner and all."

Roxy narrowed her eyes. "She's probably expecting me to."

"She *is* famous," he pointed out, giving the menu a quick glance even though he knew exactly what he was going to order.

"And she knows it." Roxy got up with such force, her chair almost fell back.

CHAPTER 13

*R*oxy's Diner. Hailey didn't recall this place at all and yet she felt sure she had been here before, that it had been some sort of restaurant. It was a vague memory, faded by time, and by the imprint of her former life.

She was about to sit down when Jackson came over and asked the server to seat her away from the tables full of people. As she settled into place and surveyed the menu, Jackson appeared deep in conversation with one of the waitresses. He was very chatty and seemed to know everyone who worked here. A tsunami of unease rolled over her as she watched him and the waitress sit down together. His casual and relaxed attitude, as if he'd forgotten that he was supposed to be a bodyguard and here for her, annoyed her.

So much for her new security detail. Jackson was too busy flirting.

She placed her order—salad and a glass of water—and when it arrived, she picked at her food while she went through the messages on her cell phone. Jackson had taken up a seat at the table with the woman and was talking away as if he was on a date, grinning impishly. He'd turn to look at her every so often, but she'd quickly look away.

She soon lost her appetite, hating him even more with each passing second. For a while on their car ride here, they had been able to talk without resorting to sniping. She had become more hopeful that she could tolerate him but seeing him now, blatantly forgetting his duty, she had half a mind to tell Val that this wasn't going to work. But that would only mean Val would send someone from LA, someone in dark shades and a conspicuous black suit. Someone looking very much out of place.

Claire had sent her a whole heap of texts and luckily, those took her mind off watching Jackson with the waitress. There were more pictures of her adorable children. Hailey suggested that they meet up again, after all, she wouldn't have long here, and this week was relatively free. Claire replied quickly saying that she was busy with the children and that she needed more time to get a babysitter.

Hailey suggested that Claire could come over to her hotel any evening that she needed to escape, and that she could bring the children with her. They could catch up in her room. It wouldn't be as much of an escape for Claire, having the children in tow, but Hailey was more than happy to help out.

Claire: I'll let you know.

Hailey: I hope you can meet up.

Jackson was eating alone at the same table he'd been sitting at. Hailey had finished her lunch, but she had no desire to sit and wait for him to finish. She got up to settle the bill, and Jackson shot up, too. He shoved his sandwich back into the brown paper bag and waited to make his payment.

Hailey walked out without saying a word to him.

She was mad at him. *Again.* And he had no idea why.

Or maybe he had a slight inkling.

He hadn't exactly checked the back exits at the diner, the way Bruce would have. He hadn't paid any attention to her, even though he'd had her in his line of sight the entire time. He'd been busy goofing around with Roxy, because this scenario had been too good to pass up.

He was still no closer to understanding what his sister had against Hailey and he had put it down to old-fashioned jealousy which pretty girls probably bore the brunt of. Roxy hadn't even gone up to Hailey. That was pretty bad, now that he thought about it.

He would apologize to Hailey, he would, and he'd do it once they were back at the hotel. No need for him to do it in front of the driver.

"Where to next, Miss Ross?" the driver asked. The tell-tale crumbs on his slacks told Jackson that the man had eaten something while they'd been in the diner.

"I'd like to go to the movie theater, please."

It didn't look as if they were going to head back anytime soon. Jax glanced towards the back, eager to strike up another conversation, an attempt at testing the waters and to determine exactly how annoyed the actress was, but her head was turned to the side and she was staring out of the window with her face set in a don't-mess-with-me expression.

Like last time, as soon as the car parked, Hailey got out and he dutifully kept his distance as he walked behind her. Having learned his lesson, he looked around, checking the surroundings, not that there was anything to be cautious about but still, he had to at least look like he was trying.

He followed her inside the Knight Movie Theater. Reed Knight had put his name on the building, fitting really, given how much money he had invested in it.

It was daytime on a weekday and there was an afternoon matinee playing. The cinema was mostly empty as he and Hailey walked in. A couple of the people working there recognized her and came over, asking if they could help her. She told them she was looking around. Then someone asked her for a selfie and an autograph. Soon after, another guy turned up and introduced himself to Hailey as the manager. Jax waited and listened to them chat about her latest movie and it reminded him that he had yet to check it out. Unlike Patrick, he'd had no interest in Hailey Ross before but after today, that had changed. The conversation soon turned polite and boring and centered on the refurbishment of the movie theater. It seemed that the guy was trying to ingratiate himself with her somehow, and he realized that this was something people did. It was something she was probably used to.

A rush of people into the lobby indicated that the matinee had finished. As the thin crowd moved to leave, some recognized her and stopped to gawk. He was immediately on his guard as news quickly spread. A wall of people came between him and Hailey.

He barreled his way through. "Hey, let's step back a little." He broke up the crowd so that there was nothing between him and Hailey. She was busy now signing autographs.

He observed from the sidelines, watched her talk and laugh with people she barely knew. She was nicer to them than she had been to him. Soon she was letting her fans take selfies with her. This was a different side to her, being so open and friendly with her fans.

The manager hovered around, then catching his eye, came over to him. "Are you a friend?" he asked.

"I'm her bodyguard."

"You look familiar."

"I'm from around here."

He kept his words short and his tone unfriendly, not wanting to lose his focus in a meaningless conversation. The manager soon took notice and moved away.

When she had taken pictures with the last fan, the manager swooped in and Jax moved closer.

"If there's anything you would like to watch, Miss Ross, we'd be delighted to have a showing for you."

She gave a false laugh. Even he could tell. "That's kind of you, but there's really no need. I'll be watching a movie here soon enough."

"Ah, yes." The manager rubbed his hands together. "Your movie premiere. We are *so* excited about that event."

"I can barely wait," she said graciously. "Thank you."

"Going back home now?" Jax asked, following her through the exit doors.

"Yes."

"Yes? Is that all I get? One-word answers? I thought we had moved on." He attempted humor, but it wasn't working.

She got into the SUV and instructed the driver to go back to the hotel. There was not one look or a word for him. It was the same when they got out at the other end. She told the driver she wouldn't be needing him today, but she had plans for more sightseeing tomorrow and that she would be down at the usual time.

She barely said a word to Jax. Engulfed in a frosty silence, they went up in the elevator and without a word, they walked to their rooms.

"Did I do something wrong?" he finally asked her just as she pressed her key card to the door and pushed it open. She let the door close again and looked at him. "If you want to flirt with all the waitresses, please do it on your own time, not on mine."

He was about to quip and ask her if she was jealous, but an attempt at humor didn't seem to be the right course of action in this moment. There was also the small point of telling her that Roxy was his sister, but he was embarrassed by Roxy's rudeness towards Hailey. He didn't feel ready to own up to that yet.

"About that," he said, taking off his baseball cap. His hair was stuck together at the top, and he ran his hand through it, ruffling it all up. "I'm sorry. I didn't know what I was supposed to do. Like I said before, this is new to me."

"I didn't realize that it was such a difficult job."

He blinked, unable to tell if she was being sarcastic or empathetic. That stone cold expression of hers gave nothing away. Red lips, with lipstick freshly applied in the car just before she walked into the movie theater likewise gave him no hint of her mood.

He forced a smile. "Keeping an eye on you isn't easy."

Her eyes narrowed, only slightly. Maybe he imagined it. Before he could think of another line to break the sub-zero atmosphere, she'd pushed her door open and disappeared.

CHAPTER 14

So, this was how it was going to be?

She got into her room, having suffered an awkward elevator ride with Jackson.

They hadn't spoken a word.

Inside her room, the flowers cheered her up. Instinctively, needing something bright, something hopeful, something cheerful, she took in a deep inhale then sat on the couch and stared at the vase on the coffee table, as if this alone could atone for the rollercoaster day she'd had.

So much for having some peaceful time off. If this first day with the new guy had taught her anything, it was that her time with him tailing her was going to be anything but peaceful.

Over the next few days, she revisited other places, including the Fitzsimmons Theater. It was strange coming back here because it elicited many memories and made her feel wistful as she found herself caught up in the nostalgia of her teen years. It was here that she had discovered her love of acting, starring in the town's Christmas pageant and rising up in the ranks from a lowly sheep before getting promoted to Mary a few years before she was discovered by the talent scout.

Jackson seemed better behaved, not as nosy and not asking her a dozen questions. He observed her as she wandered around.

A routine of sorts was forming. She texted him and the chauffeur the night before to let them know what her plans were for the next day.

Other than that, once she came back from her daily jaunts, she ate alone in her room and watched TV. Sometimes she looked through scripts.

One evening she texted Claire to see how she was, but didn't get a reply from her until well after midnight.

Claire: The little one's caught a bug. I'm changing diapers 24/7 ☹

Hailey: Oh, no. Hope he? She? Gets better soon. xx

Hailey bit her lip. She had never really thought that raising children would be so intense or so tough. Back in LA, everyone she knew with children had a live-in nanny. They also had a housekeeper. Now she was getting to see what it was like for real to bring up children without any help.

She put her phone on the table, but it rang straightaway.

"No plans today?" It was Jackson.

"No."

"So, what do I do? Hang around next door and you can tell me when you want to leave?"

"I'll summon you," she replied, unable to hold back. She could imagine his face, his quiet rage at her reply. It happened when she was around him. He brought out this diva-esque behavior, even though it wasn't what she was like. He thought she was, and she liked to play that up because it annoyed him.

He hung up.

She blanched. No one had ever hung up on her before. Frowning, she put her phone away when there was a knock on her door.

"It's me." His gruff voice, his pissed-off voice, was hard to miss. She opened the door.

"You'll *summon* me?" His face reddened as if he was going to explode.

"I was joking. Can't you take a joke?" Her voice was as cool as a cucumber.

His eyes shut for a long second, before opening again. "You call that a joke?" She had gotten to him. It hadn't been her intention but she felt playful all of a sudden, as if being here had loosened her up. In LA, she was trying to survive most of the time, wondering if she was thin enough, good enough, pretty and talented enough; even though she was a huge star, the doubts never went away.

Now her playfulness was having consequences. Jackson shook his head as if he was completely confused, though it gave her a slight sense of jubilation, especially after the way he'd behaved, smug and deliberately ignoring her at the diner while he flirted with the waitress.

She liked having the upper hand with him for once. As childish as it seemed, annoying him seemed like fun because at last, *something* seemed to get to him. Just as she was about to open her mouth to tell him that she was indeed joking he stabbed a finger towards her, his nostrils flaring. "You might be used to treating people like trash, but over here, we're polite. We don't look down on people."

His angry tone jumpstarted her shock. She wasn't used to people talking to her like that, but Jackson had done this many times. He didn't seem to care that he was an employee. "I'm not looking down on you." The idea that this was what he thought gutted her.

"No?" His nostrils flared. "You talk about summoning me, but you're not looking down on me?"

"I was joking."

"That's your idea of a joke?"

His accusation made her feel silly. Her gaze swept over him. Black tee, dark green flannel shirt, dark jeans. With his blond hair swept back like that, away from his face, all he needed was a pair of shades to complete his totally badass look.

Something tiny and electric tingled inside her. Or maybe she was cold and shivery. She pressed her lips together, not liking the way this man made her feel small. "Can't you take a joke?" It was the only thing she could think of to say. "You've spent the past few days having your subtle little digs at me."

"Like when?"

It was on the tip of her tongue, but as she stared back at him, felt the fluttery, shivery quakiness inside her, the words flew right out of her head. She couldn't think of the encounter, even though she had spent the past few days simmering with irritation at the things he'd said to her in their earlier days.

And now he had her. "When... that day in the car ...you ... you were ..."

"I was what?" he snarled.

She couldn't answer. Not when faced with that menacing look.

"I dislike people who think they're better than me," he stated.

"I don't think I'm better than you."

"No? 'Cause you sure act like it."

He had it all wrong. "I don't think I'm better than you or anyone else."

"I don't believe you." He threw his hands into the air in an act of defeat. "You know what? This isn't going to work. I can't do this. I can't work for someone like you."

She opened her mouth, shock turning her to stone. This man, the *bodyguard,* had decided he couldn't work for anyone like *her?* What did that mean?

But before she had a chance to ask him, he walked away and disappeared into his room, leaving her in complete and utter shock.

He'd walked out on her. He'd said he couldn't do this.

This was a first.

She closed the door and sat on her couch, replaying the entire scene. He was walking out on a job with her because he considered her to be too much. It hurt. Like a deep slash to her skin.

The encounter had knocked her sideways, blindsiding her as if a juggernaut had rammed into her from the side.

When her cell phone jiggled on the coffee table again, she rushed to grab it. For a crazy heartbeat moment, she thought it might be Jackson calling to apologize. Her heart sunk when she saw Val's name. That was fast. Had Jackson already told her he wanted to quit?

"Hey, how are you?" Val sounded too chirpy. It couldn't be news about Jackson.

"Great," she replied, her voice as dull as dishwater. That exchange with Jackson had deflated her spirit but Val didn't seem to notice.

"So, I've been thinking ..."

Hailey's shoulders hunched as she slunk back on the couch, cushioning the blow of whatever Val might be throwing at her. This was the way Val often started a conversation when she wanted to try to get Hailey to do something she knew she wouldn't be eager to do. Such as the time she wanted her to wear a Chanel dress to the Oscars, when Hailey had already set her mind on a dress from an up-and-coming dress designer. This was such a moment. She could feel it in her bones.

"About what?"

"The dress for the movie premiere," Val said smoothly.

Hailey let out a breath she hadn't realized she had been holding. "What about it?"

Val laughed. "You're going to need one, even in sleepy Starling Bay."

She blanched at the name. Maybe she had been a little judgmental about her hometown.

"Have you had a chance to look at the photos I sent you?"

"Sorry, I'll take a look later."

"Did you get my email?"

"Yes." She had received the notification that Val had sent her an email, but she had been so detached lately from the movie world that she hadn't gone to the trouble of opening it. "But I haven't had a chance to read it. I've been busy."

"In that sleepy town?" Val laughed. "Busy doing what?"

Trying to cover up her weary tone, not wanting to reveal that she was feeling less than stellar, she told Val what she had been up to.

"You have been busy," Val agreed. "And how is the new bodyguard?"

It didn't seem that Jackson had told her he wanted to quit. *Yet.* "He's okay."

"Okay? Is that all?"

"He's okay. He's doing what he's supposed to do."

"Good. I took a risk hiring someone I haven't seen and checked out in person but his heroic action worked in his favor."

Hailey sucked in a deep breath, not wanting to talk or think about Jackson.

"Time for you to start thinking about the dress so we can get it in time."

"It's not going to be such a big deal here, is it?" Surely not. She expected a couple of local photographers to show up.

"Whether it's a big deal or not, you still have to look like the Hollywood actress that you are."

The big Hollywood actress. She reconsidered what Jackson had said to her. Did he think she was stuck-up and believed her own hype? She tried to rack her brains for an instance which would have led him to think that she had been pompous but she couldn't. Val chortled. "I don't want you showing up in denim overalls and braids."

"That's a generalization if ever I heard one. Starling Bay is more upscale than you think."

"I'm aware of that. I'm only messing with you. Don't forget to take a look at the pictures of the dresses. I need to know which one you want so that I can get it there in time."

"I will," she promised. Nothing too glam, or too sequined, or too sexy, not here in Starling Bay. If Jackson believed she was a diva—he'd called her as much—she wasn't going to give him the satisfaction.

But why did she care so much what he thought?

"And ... uh ... look ... have you given any thought to what we talked about last time?"

"Are you still trying to coerce me into something I really don't want any part of?"

"I'm thinking about your career."

Hailey groaned.

"Think about it," Valerie pressed. "It would only be for a year."

"A year?" A shiver rolled over her. What would that mean, a year? Could she pretend to be in love for a year? Could she be dishonest to her family and her friends, and to herself?

She recoiled at the idea, shivering as if a layer of grime had suddenly spread all over her body. "I have to go," she said, suddenly standing up.

"Don't be mad at me, just think about it, that's all I'm asking."

Hailey hung up and was relieved that at least Val hadn't mentioned any names. She knew very well what she was alluding to, but the not mentioning names made it seem a part of the air, empty and invisible, which was exactly what she hoped would happen to this wild and silly idea.

It had worked out well for her to be here and not in LA. This break from her normal life was calming. It enabled her to see the tangled-up structure of her life from a distance because she couldn't see it so clearly while she was in it. Being far away gave her the space to see things differently.

Sleepy Starling Bay seemed to be just the dose of goodness she needed. Now, with the disagreement with Jackson, and Val's conversation prickling under her skin, she had no desire to stay in her room.

What she needed was to go to the beach. Or to the lake, her favorite part in all of Starling Bay. But going there would mean having to get the driver and Jackson, and he was one person she needed to avoid.

She would head for the beach and walk along the seashore looking for shells, and this time, she would go alone.

CHAPTER 15

*S*ummon?

She had some nerve.

The heck he was going to sit around waiting to be *summoned.*

He couldn't do this. No way. He didn't need to put up with some A-list megastar who behaved as if she were special.

Once again, Hailey Ross had confounded him. One minute she was tolerable and then the next she behaved like a Hollywood brat. If this was her idea of a joke, he didn't need to indulge her by putting up with it. He ran his hands through his hair, then sat down, then put his feet on the coffee table, then huffed and puffed, thinking and wondering what to do next.

Returning to his security job at the mall didn't look like an option given that he'd left them suddenly without notice and hadn't parted on good terms. He could contact Reed. Or help Roxy out in the diner.

In a fit of anger, he picked up his phone and called his sister.

"I'm busy, is it urgent?" Roxy sounded stressed, the way she always did. Maybe it wasn't a good idea for him to call her and pour out all his woes. Working for Hailey probably put him on Roxy's bad side.

"I called to see how you are." He was truly stumped. Telling her that he was thinking of quitting his new job because the actress was grating on his nerves would only rile Roxy up.

"I'm busy, but that's nothing new." She gave a dry laugh. "How are things with the actress?" Dishes and silverware crashed and clattered in the background to the point that it was getting difficult to hear anything.

"Great. It's going *great*."

"What? I can't hear you."

"GREAT," he hollered. "It's going great. Are you washing the plates, or breaking them?" He soon realized that this was going to be a pointless and thankless task, telling Roxy anything if she couldn't hear him.

"I told you I'm busy. We're getting ready for lunch. Are you bringing prima donna back?"

"You never told me why you don't like her."

"Who says I don't like her?" Roxy threw back. The clattering stopped and he assumed she had moved to her office. "You didn't even come up to her to say 'hello'," he countered.

"I was mindful of her privacy. That woman probably has people coming up to her all the time. I bet she doesn't even get to eat properly when she goes out."

He nodded, seeing things from an angle he hadn't considered before. But Roxy hadn't exactly been flattering with her comments.

"Which begs the question of why she goes out to eat," Roxy continued. "I'll bet it's because she's hungry for publicity."

"She's not."

"You would know?"

"I know more than you."

"Yeah? Something you want to tell me, Jax? How well do you *know* her?"

"I don't *know* her."

"Now you're muddling your words."

"I'm her security detail, and I've obviously come to know more about her. She's not hungry for the publicity."

"You're getting really defensive," Roxy pointed out.

"I am not." He turned the tables on her. "Is it because she's pretty that you don't like her?"

"Oh, puh-leese." Roxy roared with laughter. "You sound like you're smitten there, little bro."

"I am not."

"Why are you defending her so much?"

"Because I can't understand what you have against her."

"You have the hots for this girl," she insisted.

"Get off of it! I don't even know her."

"You just said you did!"

He did not. He didn't know Hailey Ross like *that*. His sister had it all wrong. "Nah. She's a pain in the ass."

"Oh, yeah?" Her voice had that conspiratorial tell-me-more tone. "What's she gone and done now?"

Roxy wanted gossip but he felt suddenly guilty, as if dishing the dirt on Hailey was being disloyal. He didn't owe Hailey Ross anything, but he also didn't need to complain to his sister about her. "She's done … nothing."

"I don't believe you. You hardly call me unless you need something or want to whine about something."

He was about to protest that this wasn't true, but she was right. Roxy had a read on him and there was no point lying.

"Where are you?" she asked.

"In my hotel room."

"Where's she?"

"In hers."

"Oooh, cozy," Roxy purred.

"She's in her room, and I'm in mine," he insisted.

"I heard you. No need to get defensive."

"Quit making stuff up then."

"Any chance I can come and see you one evening? Check out your fancy room at the top?"

He'd told Hailey he was quitting, but deep down, he'd spoken out of anger. He wasn't going to quit. Couldn't afford to. He needed the money, and besides, he wasn't going to leave her in the lurch. "It depends on Hailey's plans."

"Well, let me know when you can fit me in. When your actress lets you have some time to yourself."

"Ha-ha. Very funny." He hung up. That had been a waste of time.

He'd spoken in anger, telling Hailey he wanted to quit, but he had only done so because she had also spoken out of turn. They hadn't gotten off to a good start but still, he'd been hired to protect her, and it was his job. It paid well, and it had perks. He didn't have to do much but come along for the ride. It wasn't so difficult. Walking around the mall was boring and more of a pain in the butt.

This he could do.

Maybe they needed to start over and maybe he needed to apologize first. He headed to her suite and knocked on the door but there was no answer. He knocked again and looked at his watch, wondering if she might be taking a shower. Finally, he called her on her cell phone.

"Where are you?"

"Why?"

"You're not answering the door."

"Didn't you quit?"

"No. Can you please open the door, Hailey?"

"I'm afraid not."

"We need to talk."

"Talk about what?"

Jeez. She was hard work. "Hailey, quit playing around. Can you please open the door?"

"I can't, because I'm not there."

His insides hollowed out. She wasn't there? "What? Where are you?"

"At the beach."

His nostrils flared. "What the heck are you doing there?"

"Taking a walk to clear my thoughts."

"You left without telling me?"

"You quit, remember?"

He fisted his hands. "Stay there. Don't move." Grabbing his leather jacket from his room, he rushed out. He could run to the beach because it wasn't far from the hotel, but he had no idea how far along it she might be. Worried and eager to get to Hailey fast, he jumped on his motorbike, not bothering with his helmet and sped off.

Within a few minutes, he found her, a lone figure walking along the seashore. His first reaction had been relief, swiftly followed by anger. A few people were scattered around the beach, but nobody seemed to have noticed who she was, maybe because she had pulled her baseball cap down low. With her arms in her pockets, she gazed out at the sea, making him wonder what she was thinking, and why she had needed to clear her thoughts.

He left his motorbike near Kandinsky's, the ice cream parlor, and rushed over to her. His anger spilled out. "What the heck are you doing?"

She turned and jolted with surprise, her eyes widening. "You got here fast."

"What are you doing here alone?" he growled, ignoring her comment.

"I'm going for a walk. What does it look like?"

Sass. She was heavy on the sass today. "You didn't tell me."

"You said you couldn't do this."

He faced her, then took a deep inhale, hoping to calm himself down. "You put yourself at risk coming here by yourself."

She threw her hands in the air. "What did you expect me to do, Jackson? You *quit*."

His jaw tightened. "You sound like a robot."

"But you had quit. You told me." She folded her arms as if she was set on this defense, this one silly answer to explain the huge risk she had put herself in. He swallowed his pride, his frustration, his anger. If Val ever found out, and if anything had happened to Hailey, it would have been his fault.

"I'm sorry. I didn't mean what I said. I didn't quit."

"Are you sure about that?"

He stifled the retort that almost rocketed off his lips. Why could she not just accept his apology and put it behind her? Why did she need to continuously dig, dig, dig for more ways to annoy him? "Yes," he ground down on his teeth. He had to be professional. This was a job, he reminded himself. Didn't matter if she was the queen, or an actress, or a customer in a mall, his job was to make sure everything was safe and sound. "I'm sorry. I shouldn't have said what I did. You made me feel like I was an idiot."

She opened her mouth, the shock clearly visible in her expression. "Hey, Jackson … I … I don't think that at all. It wasn't my intention and I'm sorry if that's what you thought. Why would you think that?"

"People have a way of looking down on you, if they think they can."

Her forehead creased as if she didn't understand. "Is this about me asking if you owned a suit? I'm sorry. I didn't mean it like that."

"People look at me and make up their minds. They think I'm up to no good, or that I'm a certain way, like, I can't be serious or responsible."

"What? No way? What makes you say that?"

"This." He pointed to his baseball cap. "My jacket, and my bike."

"You have a bike?"

"It's in the parking lot of the hotel. I don't need to use it when I'm swanning around with you in the SUV."

"I don't think of any of those things, and I'm sorry if I made you feel that way."

He shrugged. "You probably don't have that happen to you. People look up to you, I bet, all your fans and everyone. You must be adored."

"You'd be surprised."

He was. "Yeah?"

"I've never thought of you as anything like that." She clearly wasn't going to elaborate. "I think you're stubborn, and a joker, and you're only serious when you need to be. We just got off on the wrong foot and we should have started over a few days ago at the bar, when you suggested it." Her tone was soft and she sounded as if she genuinely meant it.

He shrugged. "Okay."

"I'm sorry, too." She held out her hand, surprising him with her words and her actions. "I shouldn't have said what I did. I was joking, but I can see why it didn't come across like that."

He stared at her slim and elegant hand. Was there anything about this woman that wasn't elegant and fine? She was like a porcelain doll, and he was afraid that his roughness might crush her.

"You're not going to shake my hand?"

All he could see was the cornflower blue of her eyes. "We should start over." He slipped his hand into hers and clasped it gently for a few precious seconds. Her skin was warm and soft, and he didn't want to let go. He shoved his hands into the back pockets of his jeans.

"I was going to get an ice cream." She looked over his shoulder at the ice cream parlor. "That place never used to have that many flavors."

"Nah, it's always had that many."

She peered at him. "Sixty-four? Are you sure?"

"Well, maybe not sixty-four, but a lot. Like, definitely a lot."

"Define a lot?"

"Definitely more than thirty. They've been adding them over the years."

"That's a lot of different flavors."

"For me and my friends, Kandinsky's was always our go-to place for impressing chicks back in my teen years."

"And now?"

"Excuse me?" He was so riveted just looking at her, and enthralled in the dream-like sequence of their conversation, that all of a sudden, he wasn't sure what she was asking him.

"What do you do to impress women now?"

Was she really asking him that? He coughed, then stared at the sand, finding himself in the unfamiliar situation of not having a good answer to throw back. The problem was she was Hailey Ross. He could handle it if she were just a normal woman. He'd also know if she was hitting on him. With Hailey, he couldn't tell. Why would someone like her ever hit on someone like him?

"I don't need to impress women."

Her lips formed an 'O', and he could have kicked himself for saying something that sounded like he was bragging.

"Would you like an ice cream?" she asked quickly.

"How about I buy you one, then I'll walk ten paces behind?"

That made her laugh, and like that, in the blink of an eye, their relationship had flipped. "You don't have to walk ten paces behind."

"I need to be invisible," he said. "That's what your boss told me."

"She's not my boss, she's my agent, and what she says doesn't always go. I decide. "

They walked along the shore together, slowly heading toward the row of shops.

"I've never had to explain to someone about how to be, I mean, when they're protecting me. I didn't know what to tell you."

"I was in a mood," he confessed, "And I took it out on you."

She stared at him, but said nothing, and given the space to talk, he told her about the call from his supervisor just before she had summoned him. Because he'd been hasty in leaving, they had docked the day's wages even though he had worked most of the day and was a couple of hours from leaving.

"You lost a day's wages?"

"Yeah." It probably was nothing to someone like her, with her millions and her wealthy lifestyle. "I'm sorry. That must hurt."

"It was my fault. I wasn't very nice when I gave my notice. It was supposed to be two weeks, but Val said she wanted me to start as soon as possible and I left then and there, as soon as her contract came through."

"She shouldn't have put that pressure on you."

He waved his arm, dismissing the matter. "Don't worry about it." He had a better deal working for her, and hopefully things wouldn't be so uptight now that they had reached some sort of understanding.

"You're definitely not quitting?"

"And leave you to roam around Starling Bay alone? Heck, no."

They laughed.

He bought her an ice cream and they walked along the beach, talking about Starling Bay and the things that had changed, and the things that had stayed the same. She seemed to be happier by the time they'd finished their ice creams, and he had to admit, it was easier, smoother, more fun, getting along rather than going at each other's throats.

"You said people look down on you? I can't see that happening."

She took her shoes off and continued to walk, something he found amusing. "It's nothing."

"Can't be nothing if it makes you angry."

"It's like you say people look at you and think you're a certain way. People look at me and think I'm a certain way."

He swallowed, feeling guilty. "*You* did," she challenged, not letting him off the hook so easily. "You said I was a diva."

"I shouldn't have said that. I'm sorry."

"But you obviously thought it for you to say it, and I'm sure it wasn't just the one time."

Her acute assessment silenced him. He didn't know how to face her. She jabbed him in the ribs playfully. "It's okay. People think I'm some big-headed actress, and in my acting performances, the only range it seems I'm capable of is playing someone ice-cold and calculating, or if they put me in a pair of sexy shorts and a vest, then I'm a daring adventuress."

He laughed. "I've seen that poster of you in the mall."

"I'm sure you have."

"No, really. I have. It's in the mall where I used to work. My friend, Patrick, he's your biggest fan. He could never take his eyes off it."

She laughed. "It's a horrible poster. All those explosions behind me and me in my shades. I look like I'm leaping out of a jungle."

"I'll have to check out your movies."

"You've never seen any?" She sounded surprised.

"I haven't had the pleasure. I'll have to fix it. My sister—" he stopped. Now wasn't the time to say that his sister wasn't her biggest fan.

"Your sister?"

"Uh …" He scratched his chin. "You've seen her. She was the one in the diner the other day."

"The waitress you were talking to?"

"She's, uh … she owns that place."

"Hmmm." He could see her figuring it out.

"I thought you were flirting with her."

He shook his head vehemently. "She's my sister. I should have introduced you both."

"You should introduce me to your friend, the one from the mall."

"Patrick? He was the one who had pestered your bodyguard in the restroom that night. It's because of him that your man wasn't around when you needed him."

"I see."

"You have a signing event at the mall soon. He'll be there."

"I look forward to meeting him."

CHAPTER 16

"Do you think I need to get implants?" she asked Claire one late afternoon as they were having lunch in The Olive Tree, a restaurant in the hotel. Thankfully, it wasn't so busy. It helped that they had missed the lunch service and were too early for dinner.

Jackson sat a few tables away where he could keep an eye on her. She sometimes found herself staring at him and would then want to die of embarrassment when he'd look up and find her gaze on his.

It seemed to happen more and more as time passed and it was getting harder and harder to see Jackson as her security detail. Unlike Bruce and the others, Jackson wasn't invisible to her. She was very much aware of him in the car, in the elevator, walking around Starling Bay. She suddenly felt conscious of her every move when he was by her side.

Still, she was more relaxed now and was starting to enjoy her stay here. It even got her thinking about the idea of not returning immediately to LA after the movie premiere and spending a few more weeks here.

It wasn't just the peace and quiet of the town that called to her, but increasingly it was Jackson's company.

Claire stared at her chest. "Breast implants?"

She hadn't considered those, but it might have to come to that. "Cheek implants." Hailey put her hand to her face, wondering what it would feel like to have killer cheekbones. "Maybe a rhinoplasty." She slid her finger across her nose.

"You have a cute nose."

"I'll need a brow and forehead lift before I'm thirty."

"Whatever for?" Claire reluctantly stopped eating her apple pie. They had ordered two desserts. She had gone for a lemon meringue pie with ice cream and they were sharing. Lettuce leaves and cucumbers had long gone out of the window. She had started eating well, and didn't care about the extra inches across her waist and stomach.

"For maintenance."

"Maintenance?" Claire cried. "The maintenance of what? You already look so good. Actually, you look *great*. You make me feel like a frump." She scooped up a heap of apple pie on her fork.

"I ... what?" Hailey asked, horrified.

"It's not your fault. I feel like an overweight, untidy slob next to you."

Hailey set down her fork, feeling awful.

"It's not your fault, Hales," Claire continued, plowing into her dessert. "I feel like that because I am like that."

"No, Claire. No ... you're not. You're a gorgeous woman."

Her friend looked at her in disbelief. "You're being polite."

"You're a woman, and a mom. I see you juggling those three gorgeous children and I wonder how you get it all done."

"I don't. I mean, I *try*, and we somehow manage. It's hard work."

"I can see that, and you are amazing. You have three beautiful children and you're making a home with your family. That's incredible."

"You're making something too."

"Yes. I have a wonderful career and life and … things." She had much to be thankful for but slowing the pace down a little, walking on the beach, gazing out of the window and having time to enjoy things and be more grateful, those things were precious too.

She wondered how much more amazing it would be to have someone to share it all with. Unlike Claire, she hadn't been so lucky when it came to relationships. Hollywood wasn't the place to find something deep and meaningful. She had found that out the hard way. She'd given her heart a few times, only to have it trampled on, crushed and mangled. She loved fiercely, but the men she'd met did not.

"But, plastic surgery ..." Claire said, as if those were curse words.

"Shhhhh." Hailey put her finger to her lips and hissed as quietly as she could. Even with the low background murmur of servers and the few people chattering, she knew Jackson had the ears of a bat.

"Why on earth would you want that?"

"Look," she whispered, and pointed discreetly towards her eyes without making it that obvious. *"Lines."* The recent appearance of fine lines at the outer corners of her eyes and her forehead had almost given her a heart attack one morning. "And soon enough, my skin won't be as elastic and pumped up. I'll need *help.*"

"Help?" Claire didn't understand.

"I have to look good to get the parts. It's a constant battle."

"I'm sorry." Claire put her hand over Hailey's as an act of comfort. "I guess it's like going for a job and being really disheartened when you don't get it."

"That's exactly how it is. It's a job, like everything else, only it seems so personal because it's based on looks. Every face has to fit. I thought mine used to. Blonde hair and blue eyes, but I'm getting older and I can see how in a few years' time, the roles will dry up."

Claire almost dropped her fork in shock. "Old? At twenty-four, Hales?"

"It's not such a young age in Tinseltown."

"That's ridiculous," her friend protested.

"It's not old *old*," she emphasized. "But it soon will be." *Old* would be when she hit thirty. Heaven help her when she hit thirty-five and beyond. She would have to give it all up or find a rich man. Except she had learned that money didn't buy the things that made her happy.

"It's not old at all," Claire pointed out. "And you definitely don't need any of those implants. You'd look like one of those odd people with stretched-out faces."

Hailey ran her finger over her forehead. She had to learn to stop herself from scowling or frowning. She smothered her face with factor fifty sunblock but the LA sun was relentless. If she wasn't careful, she was going to end up with a crepey, dark-spotted leathery complexion by the time she hit her late forties.

She shuddered in horror. There would be no decent movie parts for her then, for sure. She would end up playing the hero's mother instead of his love interest.

Or the heroine's wise old mentor.

She would be done for. Taking a forkful of lemon meringue pie, she savored its sharp zesty flavor. They talked some more and ordered mint tea, which came in a pretty glass teapot with glass cups.

Every now and then, she kept looking at Jackson.

"What are you looking at?" Claire cried, turning around to gawk. She turned back to Hailey, her eyes huge like saucers.

"He's gorgeous. Have you been eye-balling him the entire time? Has he been here the whole time?"

"I have to be in his line of sight so ... I was ... I was just making sure ..."

Claire's eyes grew rounder and larger, she looked over her shoulder and back again. "In his line of sight?"

"Oh, he's my new security detail," Hailey replied casually, observing Claire's reaction with amusement.

"Your *what?*"

"My bodyguard. Will you stop staring at him?" she hissed. Claire seemed transfixed by Jackson to the point that he had noticed and raised a hand in acknowledgement. Claire waved back before turning to her. "He looks familiar."

"You don't recognize him?"

Claire shook her head.

"From the other day, at that bar we went to. Quinn's?"

"The guy who came to your rescue when that drunk guy spilled his beer?"

"That's the one."

Her friend opened her mouth, an explosion of questions clouding her expression. *"How?"* she asked finally. Hailey brought her up to speed with events.

"And you never thought to start with *that* news?" Claire made a face as if she had been badly wronged.

"I'm telling you now."

She glanced over her shoulder again.

"Will you please stop looking at him? He's going to think we're talking about him."

"We *are* talking about him. He's so dreamy, Hales. Why do you always end up with all the good things?"

"Stop that! You have all the good things. You love Rudy, you said he's besotted by you, and you have three beautiful babies."

"I know, I know that. I am blessed and I wouldn't change it for the world, but holy crab shells, Hales. You're living the life."

That's what most people thought. She was living the life, but it came at a price and this was something that most people didn't see. There were downsides to her life, but they were far outweighed by the good. She had it all, but there remained a huge gaping hole. She looked at Claire and dared to imagine what it might be like to be madly in love with someone and have a family. It wasn't something she could imagine easily.

Dinner hadn't been easy. He hadn't eaten, but instead had sipped a Coke for the longest time, sitting a few tables away from Hailey and making sure that he could see her clearly. He'd spent most of the time staring at his cell phone, pretending to be occupied, but Hailey's friend Claire had kept turning around at and gawking at him.

They had been talking about him. It was obvious, and just as obvious that Hailey kept telling her friend to quiet down. He had great hearing; his grandma used to say as much. Naturally, he had caught snippets of their conversation.

Hailey had talked about getting plastic surgery.

Seriously?

"I'd like to go to the lake tomorrow," she announced as they went up in the elevator.

"I'll let the driver know."

She shook her head. "By myself. I meant to go earlier, but I didn't get around to it. It's one of my favorite places."

"It is?"

"We used to go there for the day, my mom and dad and my sister, and we'd take a picnic and spend the day walking in the woods."

"Huh." It didn't sound anything like his idea of fun.

"I want to go alone, just to get a feel for how it used to be before."

"Alone?" he folded his arms, appraising her expression, trying to get a feel for what thoughts lurked beneath that smooth and beautiful face. "You can't go alone." When she didn't answer, he asked, "Is it really such a burden having me along?" He had started to think that they were more like friends now, and it pained him that she obviously didn't.

"It's not you. I just want to revisit it by myself. I meant to go in that first week, but then you came along and … it's not your fault," she said quickly, trying to reassure him. "With Bruce getting fired, and you being hired and the fireworks between us—"

That made him chuckle. "We can go, and you won't even know I'm there. You want to go tomorrow?"

"I'd like to go. Have you ever been?"

He shook his head. Lakes and scenery weren't his thing. Most definitely not. "I've heard of it, though."

"You've lived here your entire life, and you've never been to the lake?"

"I'm not a nature-loving guy. That's not to say I can't come to appreciate it," he said quickly. "I'll take you on my bike, if you want."

"You will?" She sounded excited, as if he had given her a piece of the moon.

"Yeah."

The smile she gave him reached her eyes and made his heart swell. It was such a simple little thing, something that others would find normal, boring, mundane—a trip to the lake on his bike.

But for Hailey Ross he felt as if he'd just told her she'd won an Oscar.

CHAPTER 17

The next morning, he took Hailey to the lake on his motorbike. He tried to focus on the bike, making sure to ride it extra carefully, petrified in case he had an accident—a crazy idea given the fact that he had never yet had any accidents. He tried not to think of her arms around his waist, tried to take his mind off the soft pressure of her body against his back.

He'd heard of the lake. Who, in Starling Bay, hadn't? But he had never been there. Staring at a lake and walking in the woods weren't the types of thing that excited him.

Once they got there, he left his bike by the parking lot near what looked like a few stores. They set off, the sound of birdsong filling the air. "I'll hang back," he told her, mindful that she had wanted to come here alone and that he was shadowing her. He couldn't imagine that kind of life, of always being in the limelight, and never having the type of quietly unnoticed life that most people did.

To think that he had once envied her. In fact, he was starting to feel sorry for her. The more he got to know her, the more he realized that the life of glamor that most people envied wasn't as wonderful as it seemed. These people really did live their lives inside a goldfish bowl, where the entire world could watch every facet of their lives. Nothing was private.

He wasn't one for being out in nature. Not deliberately. Not like this, walking through the woods aimlessly, but Hailey seemed at ease, taking her time to admire nature. He let her walk on ahead, figuring that the time to herself might be good for her.

"Walk with me," she motioned with a wave of her hand as she turned back to look at him.

"Are you sure you don't want to be alone?" He had been admiring her from behind, ever watchful, and yet deep in his own thoughts. This wasn't so bad, just him and her.

"I'm sure. I keep hearing twigs snapping behind me, and it's making me jittery." He sped up to catch up with her and they walked together. Silently at first, for the longest time. It was in this quiet that he noticed the sunshine breaking through the wall of chill. The air was cold, the ground icy, but every now and then, tiny slivers of sunlight would come through and the warmth gave him something else to be grateful for. After a while he caught glimpses of the glittering lake shimmering through the trees and they soon came to a clearing. Here they could see the lake in its entirety, stretching out before them and sparkling under the sun. Light reflected and bounced off the surface of the water.

He had to agree, it wasn't so bad. It was peaceful. The twittering of birds punctured the pin-drop silence. "Happy?" he asked, glancing at Hailey. Her eyes were closed and she seemed to have disappeared into her own private world. It was only when she opened her eyes that she caught him staring at her. It was so blatantly obvious that he couldn't cover it, or pretend he'd been staring at something else. He felt compelled to say something.

"You look so beautiful." But *that* hadn't been the thing he'd meant to say. He hadn't thought. The words had tumbled out, because she was beautiful. "I mean as "As in peaceful and calm."

He cleared his throat, not wanting her to think he was a creep, or that he was hitting on her.

She nodded.

Then, because it needed to be said, "You don't need to get that stuff done, the plastic surgery or the implants."

Her eyes went round. "You heard that?"

"I tried not to, but … I couldn't help it."

She looked embarrassed; her cheeks turning pink. He didn't want her to feel bad. "You're perfect the way you are, Hailey, and don't let anyone tell you otherwise."

The fresh air was getting to him and making him say silly things. Things which under normal circumstances he would never have said.

She wrung her hands together. "I can't believe you heard us. What do you have, bionic ears?"

He chuckled. "My Grandma used to think so. I wasn't trying to listen in, I swear." He didn't want her to feel bad. Seeking to reassure her, he said, "You're perfect. *All* of you. You shouldn't even be thinking about things like that."

She shifted from one foot to the other and stared at the ground. "It's kind of you to say that, but in Hollywood, if you saw all the other actresses, you would see how high the bar is."

"Then maybe you have to figure out if that's the kind of bar worth reaching for."

She took a few paces towards the lake and gazed at it in silence. Looking at her back, seeing her hair billowing behind her, she became someone else. Not a stranger anymore, not a diva, not even an actress. Just Hailey.

A friend.

Someone shy and quiet and friendly and sweet. Nothing like how he had imagined she might be. "Look, Hailey, I don't mean to overstep my mark. I'm sorry that you feel embarrassed but I want you to know, you don't need that stuff."

They both stood at the edge of the lake, looking straight ahead. He didn't want her to be uncomfortable, and right now he wasn't talking like her protector, but her friend; because he cared, and someone needed to tell her the truth.

Though he was conscious of overstepping his boundary, hers wasn't the expression of someone who wanted him to stop—unlike with the drunk at the bar the first day he'd met her. "You say all the nicest things."

"Someone has to."

"So?" She waved her hand at the lake. "What's your verdict."

"It's not so bad."

"Not so bad?" she cried. "Is that the best you can do?"

He nodded, as if weighing up his answer. "It's really very pretty. I can see why you like it here." It was quiet, and maybe being with nature made people go all trippy, because he was saying all sorts of things he wouldn't normally have said. Roxy would think he'd lost his mind. "This is one of your favorite places?"

"My absolute favorite."

"I thought you had airs and graces. I thought you were stuck-up."

"Stuck-up?"

"Obviously I was wrong."

She smiled.

"We didn't exactly get off on the right foot," he said.

"No."

They watched the lake in silence, lost in their thoughts. He wanted to say more, but he was reminded of his place. And yet the lines were blurring—this ease of being around her, the types of conversations they were starting to have, these were different now. He wasn't sure if this new turn in their friendship was something he imagined, and he wondered if she felt the same.

They walked back through the forest, and returned to the

parking lot. "Stores," she said, as if noticing them for the first time. "Some of these weren't here before." She started to walk towards them. "Ella Ray's Mystic and Magic? That's new." He followed her as she peered inside into the shop windows. "Do you believe in that stuff?"

"I don't know what I believe, sometimes."

"Why don't you go inside, if you're curious?"

She appeared to consider it when the door to the gift shop opened and the biggest dog he had ever seen strained at his leash. He looked as if he was going to charge at them. Jackson put himself in front of Hailey.

"Steady, Spart," the owner said. He seemed to be struggling to keep the dog under control. The Great Dane strained at the leash, his tongue lolling out as he looked ready to sprint across the fields. "Oh, hey," the man said. There was something familiar about him as they stared at one another.

"Hi," said a woman who appeared by the man's side.

He and Hailey both said 'hi' back.

Hailey walked up to them. "Mind if I pet him?"

"Go ahead," the woman told her. "He's not as scary as he looks."

A flicker of knowing in the man's expression told Jax that he recognized Hailey. He expected the couple to whip out a notepad and ask her for an autograph or a photo, but surprisingly, they just smiled and said nothing, letting Hailey pet the dog.

"Hey there," she purred. "You're gorgeous, aren't you?" She petted him some more.

"He looks like he's waiting for you to cut him loose," said Jax.

"He knows it's time for his daily walk," the man answered. "I'm Dylan, by the way, and this is Merry."

Jax and Hailey introduced themselves and she gave the dog a final friendly pat. "I won't keep you."

"It was nice to meet you," Merry said, as they turned to go.

"Nice to meet you," Hailey replied.

"Oh, and welcome back," Dylan said. Then they were gone, heading towards the woods.

"They make a nice couple," Hailey mused, her voice sounding all dreamy.

"Yeah. They seem like it. Do you want to look around the gift shop?"

"Maybe next time."

"Do you want to head back?"

She nodded.

"Was it okay riding on the bike?" he asked, handing her the helmet.

She chewed her bottom lip, looking uneasy.

"What?" Maybe she didn't like sitting so close to him or having to put her arms around his waist. Maybe he had it wrong, because these had been the very things that had been the highlight for him.

"Insurance."

"Excuse me?"

"I'm not sure Val would approve. I think I need to be insured or something. I'm not supposed to do spontaneous things."

Heck. He hadn't even thought of that. He was insured, but obviously not for the likes of Hailey Ross. "I can call the driver if you want him to take you ba—"

"No!" She shook her head. "No, forget I said that."

"But if we have an accident."

"We won't. Pleeease," she begged.

He chewed it over. She didn't do spontaneous things. "I'll just ride carefully." Knowing she had been behind him, he had been anyway.

~

A thrill of dangerous excitement throbbed through her veins. In her chest, she could feel the reverberations of her pounding heart.

She prayed that Jackson couldn't hear them. Riding with him, like this, with her hair blowing out as the wind shredded through it, she felt free.

The visit today had brought back memories of her younger days, when she would come here with her family and spend the day walking through the woods then having a picnic by the lake. Those had been golden days.

Great days.

Days free from stress and worry.

Childhood days, when the pressure and the eyes of so many hadn't been on her. Leaving Starling Bay and going to Hollywood had seemed like such a big deal to her in those teenage years. It was a big deal no matter what age, but this return had made her see things differently and she felt slightly jaded now about her current career path. It was almost as if the color had faded a little and taken the shine off what she had thought was a great life.

Jackson had been sweet, too, and maybe that had made all the difference. Him talking about her looks and her not needing to get plastic surgery; that had been a compliment, yet it had felt deeper than just surface level kindness. She hadn't been able to look at him, and getting on the motorbike to come home, she had felt a little shy. The way in which she knew him had started to change. Something about their relationship had shifted.

She preferred to believe that they were friends and not that he was her bodyguard. What made this situation difficult was the fact that he happened to be her age, and with looks to die for.

Had he always been this handsome? Had it been so dark at that bar, had she been too shaken by the drunk to notice it when they had first met?

She was still lost in these thoughts as they made their way up in the elevator.

"Thanks," she said as they went to their respective doors. She didn't want him to leave. She didn't want the day to end now and she hesitated before sliding the key card.

Ask him.

He seemed to wait, as if he too were loathsome to go in. "It was a good day, huh?"

She nodded. The question danced on her lips. *Ask him if he wants to get something to eat.*

"See you tomorrow."

It was too late.

She went into her suite and closed the door, then leaned against it, wondering why she had chickened out. It would only have been dinner. Room service. Nothing more to it, but now it was too late.

CHAPTER 18

Starting over and calling a truce had been the right thing to do despite the fact that this was a situation she had never been in before with her previous bodyguards. They spent the next few days walking along the beach, eating ice cream and talking, and it felt as if she and Jackson were now fast friends. The atmosphere between them had lightened and was so much more pleasant.

He never again mentioned anything about quitting.

The film crew arrived and took up residence on another floor of The Grand Hotel. Hailey had met with them soon after and had gotten to know Abe O'Sullivan, the TV anchor who would be interviewing her. The plans were for the documentary to be filmed in the Fitzsimmons Theater.

Clips of the interview would be interspersed with footage of her visiting many of the places that held special memories from her time here. Some of these were places she had already visited with Jackson. She wasn't going to share the lake or the woods with Abe and his crew. That place was sacred.

She missed having time to herself to do as she pleased, and she especially missed it being just her and Jackson. He was always by her side, within earshot, yet discreet and almost invisible. If there was any saving grace, it was that she was only needed for a few hours a day, and the filming would be over by early afternoon and after that she was free to do as she wanted.

Abe was good at making her feel at ease. His interview style was easygoing and he had prepared her by giving her a list of questions he was going to ask. These were casual, not hard-hitting questions he asked her, and when she'd had a quick look through the list, she felt better. She could handle these types of questions.

One day, a makeup artist had been touching up her makeup so that she wouldn't look so washed out under the glare of the camera lights. As she opened her eyes, there had been a moment when she had caught Jackson staring at her. It was one of those electric shock moments that made her jolt, and her skin tingled with electricity. It happened more as the days passed. The looks between them were freighted with something solid.

She tried not to think about it as she sat facing Abe across the stage, trying to remember the answers she had prepared but knowing that Jackson was there, within earshot, listening to her, made her more self-conscious than ever.

She had been quiet in the car on the way home and Jackson seemed to respect her need for solitude.

Over the following days, there were visits to the beach, and the new movie theater where she was asked the same old questions about whether she had ever dreamed that she would one day be on the silver screen.

Because he was always close by, Jackson heard everything, and she felt more self-conscious opening up to him than she did to the TV host. As she shared parts of her life story, it felt strange that Jackson knew these things about her.

By the end of the first week's filming, she hankered for normal company, away from the lights and the probing questions. Feeling lonely one evening, she invited Claire over, and told her to bring her children. She had bought a few things for the children in readiness for their visit and sent the driver to go and fetch them.

"Are you sure?" Claire asked, even as she barreled into the hotel suite with a baby in her arms and two toddlers around her legs: her mini entourage.

"I am sure. Hey, kids." She smiled at them as two of them hid behind Claire, sticking to her as if they were another leg each, and she held the baby in her arms. She also had a lot of luggage with her and Hailey wondered why she needed so many bags.

"Say hello," Claire told them.

The children shyly did as they were told. The baby cooed. His big eyes reminding her of green marbles. "Come here, you little cutie." She couldn't help it and reached out for him. To her surprise, he put his arms out for her to take him.

"This is a first," Claire cried. "He doesn't go to anyone. This is Baby Jack," she said, taking the baby's coat off carefully as Hailey held him.

"Baby Jack." Hailey hugged him, loving the alien feel of a baby in her arms. She held him to her chest and breathed in his lovely scent. It was warm and cottony, like talcum powder and fresh laundry. The baby cooed in response.

She hadn't picked up a baby in years. Or ever. She tried to think. Actor friends who had babies never seemed to look after them, and the children were always with the nanny. Her own sister didn't have any children, so this was something new to her.

Claire shrugged out of her coat and helped the children out of their coats. "And this is Cicely. Say 'hi,' Cicely." Her daughter stuck two fingers in her mouth and managed a shy 'hi''.

"Hi, sweetie." Hailey moved the baby to her other hip. "And who's this?" she asked, her voice going all gooey at the little man who had one arm entwined between his mom's legs, and the other holding a tiny toy car.

"Freddie," Claire crouched down to his level. "What do you say?" Freddie didn't say a word. "Freddie, honey. What do you say?"

"Aw, don't make him." Hailey gave the child a sunny smile as he stared up at her with suspicious eyes. Big, beautiful eyes, but suspicious all the same.

"Fine example he's going to set for the others."

"Hey, wanna see what I got you?" Hailey asked. The toddlers nodded and followed her. She pulled out the bag of goodies she'd bought them earlier in the week. "They're yours. Come on and take them out."

Claire walked around the room, her jaw falling open. "This is *gorgeous.*"

"Thank you."

"It's really lovely," Claire sighed. Hailey wondered what her friend would make of the many luxury hotels she had stayed in before. Some of them had left her spellbound by their expensive décor and out-of-this-world luxury.

Still holding the baby, she emptied out the contents of the bag since the children wouldn't.

"What do you have for them?" Claire asked, coming over.

"Oh, nothing really. Just a few things I picked up. I wasn't sure what they would be into. I wasn't sure of their ages."

"The baby's fourteen months, and Cicely is three and Freddie is?"

"Four!" Freddie held up three fingers proudly.

"That's three, honey." Claire held up four of her fingers.

"Four," her son cried again, still holding up three fingers.

"I give up." Claire walked around still examining the suite. "You can set him down," she told Hailey. "He can walk."

"I like holding him. I don't get a chance to cuddle babies much." With Jack balanced on her lap and with one arm firmly holding him in place, she watched the children grab their coloring books and pencils and toys. "Do you want to check that these are safe?" she asked Claire.

"Thanks, Hales. That's so sweet of you, but you didn't have to get them anything." Claire sank onto the couch and gave the books and toys a quick once over.

"I wanted to. I've been looking forward to meeting your gorgeous children."

"Aww. Thanks. That's so sweet of you, and to have us all over."

"I'm glad you could come." She propped the baby on her lap, with him sitting facing her and she held his tiny little hands. He was gorgeous, plump and soft, with the cutest smile.

Claire sighed loudly, curling her legs on the couch. "He's yours for the entire evening."

"Oh, I don't intend to let go of him. By the way, we're having room service. Would that be okay with you?"

Claire looked at her as if she had won the jackpot. "Room service?" she echoed, as if it were some magical, mystical thing.

She told Claire all about what she had been up to during her time here. She fed the baby some mushed up food that Claire had brought along with her, and once the baby had eaten, she let him crawl around on the floor. Luckily, the suite was more or less childproof, and when the baby strayed too far, his older brother and sister were on the case, like overprotective siblings.

Over chicken Alfredo, and a bottle of wine for her and Claire, and pizza and chips for the children, the two friends caught up.

The kids suddenly started to make a commotion. It was the loudest sound Hailey had heard in a long time.

"I want it!" one screamed.

"No, *I* want it!" screamed another. Then, another loud scream. The piercing shriek went right through Hailey's ears. She jumped up, scared that one of them had injured themselves. "What is it? What's going on?" she cried, looking at Claire helplessly. Her friend seemed too relaxed on the couch, with a glass of wine in one hand.

"Cicely, give Jack back his toy," their mother instructed. The little girl pouted. "Honey, give it back, *now*." Claire's voice was firm, but Cicely held onto something in her hand, her chubby fingers gripping it tightly. They were fighting over the plastic lion. She had bought them a small pack of animals, not thinking that they might not share.

Claire started to set down her glass on the table. "You sit back," Hailey told her. "I've got this." She could see that tonight was a rare night for Claire, and she wanted her friend to enjoy it. Besides, she was getting hooked on little Jack. She scooped him up in her arms and shushed him, expertly fishing out a toy tiger from the same pack of jungle animals.

"What did I tell you, Cicely?" Claire cried.

"It's okay," Hailey hushed her. "He's got something else now, haven't you, Jack?" she pulled the tiger away and listened to him gurgle with joy as he tried to reach it with his chubby little hands. "Is this what you want?" she cooed, jiggling around with him. She brought the tiger back within his reach. He grabbed it and rocked against her with excitement. "Whoa." Hailey held onto him with both arms firmly around him. The child had almost rocked right out of her arms. This was all so new to her.

"He likes you," Claire observed, refilling her wine glass. Hailey smiled. It was just as well since she had the driver on standby to drop them all back later. So, this was what being a mother to three children was like.

The two older children were polite and sweet, and busy. Her coffee table and the floor were strewn with markers and coloring pencils and books and papers.

A knock on the door startled her and she walked over with the baby, thinking that it might be room service coming early to remove the dishes. She opened the door to find Jackson, his brows furrowed together, peering at her.

"Gooo—goooo!" Jack gurgled, putting the tiger in his mouth.

"No, honey, that won't taste nice. No, don't do that."

"Company?" Jackson's gaze fell to the baby.

"Sorry. Were we making too much noise?"

"I was wondering what was going on."

"Well … *hello!*" A slightly tipsy Claire stared at Jackson with a silly grin on her face. "Why don't you come on in and join us?"

Hailey suppressed a grin and waited for Jackson's reaction. He held out his hand. "We've met before, I believe."

"We certainly have." Claire gripped his hand as if she had no intention of letting it go. "You're the one who saved Hailey from that idiot."

"Yes, ma'am."

"Don't ma'am me," Claire shot back, making a futile attempt to run her hand through her hair. "I might look like I've aged— this is what having kids does to you—but I'm not much older than you, I bet."

Jackson gave her a sympathetic smile.

"Come on, come in," Claire insisted, taking a hold of his arm.

"I should go."

Claire made a puppy-dog face. "Does he have to go? Can't he stay?"

"He can't stay. That's not what he does." It would be better if Jackson left before Claire said something embarrassing.

"Don't go!" Claire cried, as Hailey closed the door on him. "Why can't he come in? He's your bodyguard, isn't he?"

"You're a married woman!" Hailey hissed.

"But he's so cute!"

"You're married!"

"That doesn't change the fact that he's cute!" Claire traipsed back to the couch sorrowfully. Hailey joined her and settled the baby on her lap. "How can you flirt with him?"

"I'm *looking*, Hales. Not going to do anything. Just admiring and appreciating a thing of beauty."

"He is cute," she agreed. He was rugged, but not in a rough way. He wasn't chic, or elegant, or refined. He'd told her once that people looked at him a certain way, that they found him rough and hard. She did, too, but, as she was beginning to find out, these were the qualities which attracted her to him. The baby squirmed out of her lap, and she let him go. "Have you ever seen him before?" she asked casually, picking up her wine glass.

"How would I know him? I barely go out, and I wouldn't forget a face like his."

Hailey held back a grin. "Doesn't everyone know everyone else here?"

"Hyacinth Fitzsimmons is the only one. Everyone knows her, and she knows everyone."

The name rang a faint bell. "You mean the woman in charge of the Christmas pageant? That old battle axe is still around?"

"Yes, and she has her nose in everyone's business." They burst out laughing. Hyacinth Fitzsimmons wasn't easy to forget. She seemed to head up all the committees in town, and she was always sticking her nose into the Christmas pageant.

"Let's not talk about Hyacinth," said Claire. "I want to know what it's like having a bodyguard who looks like an actor."

"Stop it." Hailey tried to look serious, but it was hard because just thinking about Jackson made her smile.

She looked so different with a baby in her arms. More relaxed and carefree, but she had also lowered her guard lately, and she seemed more chilled out to him than ever. Even so, this was a nice change, Hailey being surrounded by a chorus of noisy children. He liked casual and happy Hailey better than stressed-out Hailey.

When his cell phone buzzed in his shirt pocket, he fished it out and was surprised to see that it was Val.

"Hey, Val."

"Just a quick heads-up. Are you all set for the event at the mall?"

All set? "What do I need to do?"

"Nothing, except get her in and out of there fast."

This directive surprised him, since Val hadn't given him much instruction other than to 'guard her well' before. "Anything I need to know?"

"Just some fanmail from an overzealous admirer."

Fanmail. Hailey had hinted at this before. "Same guy?"

"She told you?"

Val sounded surprised. "Yeah, she told me. What is it?" Something was going on, and Val was trying to sound not so bothered. The fact that she had hinted at this now told him that something *was* going on.

"It's only harmless fanmail—"

"It can't be harmless if you're worried about it." She had made him worried. He drew his lips back in a snarl; the idea of anyone wanting to cause Hailey harm made him uneasy. It wasn't going to happen, not on his watch.

"There are a lot of sad and lonely people in the world, Jax. They're dreamers, shall we say."

"What makes you think they're not deluded or sick enough to think that their thoughts aren't real?"

"Because this is common. If we got worried about every single item of fanmail from every oddball, I wouldn't sleep."

He didn't think he was going to sleep. "Are you sure you don't need to send someone?" He worried that his level of security—no guns, no real training, wouldn't be enough to protect her properly.

"No one knows she's not in LA."

"They will once the documentary airs."

"That's not happening for another month, and she'll be back after the movie premiere. Make sure she leaves the mall as soon as the signing is over. And stay by her side. I've arranged the entire setup with the publicity department at the mall."

He chortled. Publicity department at the mall. That would likely be the same person taking care of a whole heap of other things. "I'll make sure she's in and out fast."

CHAPTER 19

"What made you go into acting?" Abe asked.

"I've always been a shy person--"

"You, shy?" Abe cried in disbelief. Jax watched and listened from the sidelines as Abe interrogated Hailey. As usual, she was on the stage sitting across from him, fully made up again, looking striking, and smiling as she carefully considered her answers.

"Yes, shy. Very shy. I am even now."

"I don't believe it."

She giggled. "I am, in real life, and so I discovered that when I was on stage, being someone else, I could come out of my shell. I could be anyone I wanted. I loved that."

It pinched at his insides, made his rage simmer slowly as he watched this man ask her all sorts of questions.

This is show business, he reminded himself.

She wants this. She was doing this in order to plug her latest movie. He forced himself to remember that this documentary would give her more publicity, but he had also started to know a little of the real Hailey Ross and that she wasn't the person everyone saw. Underneath, peeling back the layers slowly, she was a gentle soul, a woman full of insecurities.

His eyes were being opened slowly. Standing around in Hailey's shadow with the film crew following her every move and that interview guy talking to her as if he was her best friend, and that annoyed him the most.

He saw this exchange as an interrogation, dressed up as a TV interview. The questions continued and she answered them as he fired them at her. She was always the consummate professional, but he felt that the questions were becoming more personal.

"Do you have any regrets?" Abe asked. Hailey seemed to close up. To the cameraman, and to Abe and to the entire crew watching, they might have been fooled by that smile, but he wasn't. She looked comfortable, but opening up wasn't something she was happy to do.

"Regrets?" He could tell she was buying time. A flash of discomfort flickered across her face. This wasn't a question Abe had told her he'd be asking.

"Regrets about anything?" he asked, prying deeper into her life. A couple of times he sensed she was uncomfortable, her eyes surveying the crowd—which, because it wasn't being done in front of an audience, was comprised of only him and the film crew. Did she feel coy and sensitive because of him?

"I don't call them regrets, when things don't work out, I mean, to me they're lessons to be learned."

"When what doesn't work out?" Abe probed. The guy made Jackson's fists curl.

Back off, dude. Leave her alone.

"Are you talking about relationships?"

Jax's hands turned to fists. Abe was one slimy snake.

"I'm talking about movie roles, Abe."

"Movie roles?"

Hailey nodded. "I've wanted roles that would help me to expand my acting range, and that hasn't worked out the way I wanted. I seemed to be pigeonholed into a certain character." Jax could tell she was hoping Abe would ask her more questions along those same lines, but he didn't. He nodded quickly, as if he wanted to move on to meatier things, as if this wasn't the direction he wanted the interview to go in. "Anything else? Any other goals or something else you wanted to achieve?"

"You make it sound as if I'm at the end of my career, Abe." She flashed him a huge smile.

Abe turned to the camera and gave a tight smile, a defeated smile. He wasn't going to get anything out of her today. The small talk continued, and soon after they called it a wrap.

They were done for the day. Today the filming was wrapping up slightly earlier because she had the event at the mall later on.

Damn it.

He had meant to call Patrick to tell him that he might not be able to introduce him and Hailey. She had happily agreed, but after Val's call, Jackson was eager to put Hailey's safety first and he was determined to get her in and out of the mall as fast as possible. He reached for his cell phone, hoping to let Patrick know upfront rather than to let his friend down again for the second time when Hailey charged towards him.

"Everything okay?" he asked, seeing the look on her face.

"I need to get out of here."

He led the way and opened the door to the SUV which was parked outside.

"Back to the hotel," he told the driver. He glanced over his shoulder, but Hailey was busy on her phone. Later as they got into the elevator, he asked her how she put up with those questions from Abe. "Don't you find them intrusive?"

"You sensed it too?"

"He was getting personal towards the end."

"He wasn't supposed to. I told Val to ensure he stayed on topic."

"I could tell you weren't comfortable."

She looked at him, a worried expression creeping across her face. "Was it obvious?"

He shook his head. "Not to anyone else. You're professional and poised. You don't give anything away, Hailey. You're always performing."

Her expression softened, as if he had somehow given her permission to be. "Then how could you tell?"

What was he supposed to say to her? He could tell because he was in tune with her moods and her mannerisms. Because he had come to know every expression on her face. Because he sensed when she was angry, or subdued, when she held back, and when she shared. He had come to read her body language not only because he was naturally good at these things, because his jobs had taught him to read people, not because of the time he spent with her, but it was more than that. He understood her.

"How?" she asked, and he realized he hadn't yet given her an answer.

"Because I'm good at reading people," he managed to say, and hoped that she believed it.

"I didn't like those questions at the end."

"I know. That guy was starting to annoy me." The elevator doors zinged open and he let her step out.

Hailey looked at him in surprise. "He was starting to annoy you? Why?" He stopped by her door, gazed at her, tried not to fall into those big blue eyes.

"I ..." he shrugged. "I don't know. I guess I got mad at him for asking you questions you didn't want to be asked."

She laughed. "That's so sweet, but why did *you* get mad?"

"I hated that he was being so nosy."

She sighed and brushed a hand across her neck. In the silence that dragged out, neither of them moved. He didn't want to leave her. He wished things could go back to how they'd been when he used to go around with her, when it had been just the two of them.

"I should ..." he forced himself to take a step back towards his door. "I should, uh ... what are your plans?"

"I'm going to order room service and then get ready for the mall signing."

"The mall signing," he echoed, wondering if he should ask her if she wanted to get some lunch together, but then he reminded himself of who he was, and who she was. And that this was nothing more than his job.

"The signing is at seven. When do you need me to be ready by?"

It was almost on the tip of his tongue to ask her. They had plenty of time. For lunch, for more talking. This is a job, he reminded himself. He had to keep his distance. "Six thirty is good."

"Six thirty?" she asked.

"Yeah, or do you need more time?"

"No, that's fine."

Mindful of her insecurities, he added, "I didn't mean that you needed more time. You don't need any time. You're perfect the way you are. You could go dressed in that."

She chewed on her lip and he stopped abruptly, aware that he was blabbering. "I'll see you at six thirty."

CHAPTER 20

*D*id she need more time?

Jackass.

You're perfect the way you are.

What a wuss. If Roxy had heard him say that, she would have doubled over with laughter.

But it was true. Hailey was perfect in every way and the fact that he had never said that or thought that about any woman he'd met so far told him something.

But she was also out of his league.

He spent the next few hours working out in his hotel room, then showered and changed. He had no idea about mall signings and what they entailed, but he wanted to look smart. Showing up in his jeans and biker jacket was no longer good enough. He wanted to take it up a bit and look more presentable.

He'd bought a suit to wear, thinking it was high time he spruced himself up instead of wearing casual clothes. He didn't want to do a 'Bruce', but he could do better than his dark jeans and shirt.

A few minutes before six thirty, he paced around outside Hailey's door. When a few moments had passed, he got worried and knocked on the door. When she didn't answer, he pulled out the key card he had to her suite, something that Val said was a normal arrangement.

"You have a key to my room?" she asked, her eyes huge with shock as he opened the door. But he was too stunned by her appearance to answer. She had surprised him yet again--but that wasn't the reason he was speechless. He'd expected her to be in a dress, but she had on a smart yet casual cream-colored pantsuit and t-shirt. She was glowing. "Jackson. How did you get the key to my room?"

Her harsh tone soon snatched him out of his spell of admiration. "Uh... Val arranged for me to have it."

"How did I not know this?"

His mouth fell open. He wondered how much stuff Val kept from her. "I don't know. She said Bruce had a spare key card as well. Didn't you know?"

"No, I didn't."

"If Val says I need it, then I guess I have to have it." He wasn't going to walk in on her on purpose. "All set?" he asked, changing the subject quickly.

"Yes."

They got into the elevator and he noticed her gaze sweeping across him. He was trying hard not to make it so obvious that he was doing the same.

"You look great," he told her.

"So do you. I like your suit."

"Thanks."

It fell silent in the elevator. He had so much he wanted to say but she seemed annoyed. He hoped it wasn't because of the key card. It was strange how quickly he picked up on her moods, and how much he longed to talk to her. "Are you worried about the signing?"

"I'm looking forward to it. It will take my mind off things."

"Take your mind off anything in particular?" Did she know that Val was worried? Had she heard of the worrisome fanmail? He couldn't even ask her without getting her all worried.

"Movie stuff. Silly stuff," she said, telling him nothing. The elevator doors opened, and as they walked out to a crowd of people who began taking photos with their cell phones.

He moved in front of her, shielding her from the crowd who were made up of adolescent teenagers, chanting her name.

People cried out her name, shouting requests for taking pictures with her and for her autograph.

"Can I get an autograph?" someone asked, and almost grabbed her arm.

"Sorry." He put his hand out, as if to keep the small crowd away and to clear a path so that Hailey could follow.

She tapped him on his arm. "I don't mind signing a few autographs."

"Just a few minutes." He didn't want to risk being late for the mall.

She was soon surrounded by groups of eager fans, mostly girls, he noted, feeling better at seeing that. Still, he continued to watch the crowd with more diligence now, looking on as Hailey smiled and happily signed autographs whenever a pen and notepad were thrust in her face. She did it all with grace and composure.

As he glanced around the hotel lobby, he noticed that more people were beginning to hear the commotion. Some started to head towards them. Soon, he alone wouldn't be able to effectively shield her from crowd surge.

At least at the mall, Hailey would be behind a table and the mall's security would be at hand to keep the crowds at bay. He'd called his supervisor and checked and found a complete role reversal in him having to call as a client rather than an employee.

"Come on," he told her as she started to pose for more pictures with fans. "We have to go."

"Just a few more."

"Quickly, Hailey. We need to go."

He waited for a few minutes, then reached for her hand, since she didn't seem to get the hint, and he almost tugged her along with him. The SUV had pulled up outside and he quickly bundled her in. Hailey sat back, smoothing down her hair. "That got heavy fast."

"People are slowly finding out that you're here."

She groaned. "There won't be any peace now."

"It probably won't be so bad tomorrow," he said, trying to reassure her. "The news must be spreading quickly that you're making an appearance at the mall."

She looked out of the window, the way she always did when she didn't want to face things. A short while later her cell phone rang. He was used to her ringtone; a catchy pop tune that had been in the charts a few months ago. She was still a young girl at heart, even though listening to her talking to Abe made her seem sometimes wiser beyond her years.

"We're on our way," he heard her say. The conversation turned to the documentary. It sounded as if Val was at the other end.

"I didn't get it?" he heard her say. She sounded disappointed. He looked in the rearview mirror, feeling her hurt as if it were his. "That's not fair. I didn't even know she had auditioned for it." She sighed out loud. "When did you find out?" Another groan. "That's not fair. That's just not fair."

He listened to the exchange, straining his ears to hear every single word. It sounded as if she had missed out on a part she wanted. They drove in silence the rest of the way. When the car pulled up at the back of the mall, he got out first then rushed over to her door and opened it for her. "Everything okay?" He wanted her to open up to him, even though right now wasn't the perfect time.

The sadness in her eyes told him it was anything but okay. "Not really. No. Let's get this over with." She looked defeated. This wasn't the Hailey he had come to know, the one who gave her fans all of her and put on a brave face no matter what was going on in her personal life.

They were met by someone from the mall's management team. Jax recognized the guy who looked as if he couldn't do enough for Hailey. He shook her hand, and stared into her eyes, and Jax knew the guy was enthralled.

He didn't like the way the man gawked at her; the man was old enough to be her father. He glanced sideways at Hailey, but she appeared undeterred, as if she had put on a mask and no one or nothing could penetrate it.

Out of curiosity, he had looked her up online a few days ago and had spent an entire evening reading up about her, and poring through the many photos online, of her at red carpet events, her on the arms of many famous Hollywood heartthrobs.

It hadn't been easy looking through them all and seeing her other life. The only relief he'd felt came from her name not being linked to anyone at the moment aside from an actor guy she had given an award to, the new big guy in the summer hit—a guy called Big Rock. It didn't look as if they were an item.

A roar erupted as they walked through the double doors which led onto the floor of the mall. Glancing to the side, he saw a huge crowd of people lining up behind temporary erected metal guards keeping the fans at bay. A group of security guards flanked at either side, creating a tunnel through which she could walk safely to get to a table which had been set up for her in a section of the mall.

He guessed she would be doing her signing there. There seemed to be many more posters of her new movie all around the mall. He stared at her in her shorter than short shorts and her skimpy vest and looked away. These were the things that would lead to more sleepless nights.

Looking back to that first day when Patrick had told him that she would be returning to Starling Bay, he couldn't believe that he had been so blind, or so dismissive of her.

"Hail-lee, Hail-lee, Hail-lee!" The crowd chanted and whooped for joy. He estimated that maybe up to five hundred people were here. The size of this crowd all gathered in one area made him uneasy.

Patrick was standing over near one of the pillars, and winked at him before nodding at Hailey. It was a don't-you-forget look. Jax slapped a hand to the back of his neck in frustration. He had forgotten to warn his friend that he wouldn't be able to make the introduction.

Hailey spent the next few hours switching on her brightest smile and talking cheerfully to fans who lined up and approached her at the table one by one. Her publicity company had made up bags of movie-related merch, with a postcard inside that she signed.

What he wasn't prepared for was the sight of Abe and his crew. They showed up halfway through, probably wanting to get some footage for the documentary. He nodded at him in acknowledgment, since he was a regular around the set now.

But he could tell. Despite that thousand-watt smile, Hailey didn't look as if her heart was in it.

The evening passed without any major problems. How she managed to sit at that table, smiling continuously and talking to people who were nothing more than strangers for so long, he didn't know.

Mindful of Val's instructions to get her back immediately, he rushed to her side as soon as the event ended. The mall doors had been closed earlier to control the crowd and people were being directed to leave through another exit.

"Come on, we have to go," he said, standing by her side.

Abe stepped in. "Could we get some footage? Some words from you for the documentary?"

"Don't you have enough?" He'd seen them filming her during the signing.

Abe shot him an angry look. "I want to get a few words from Hailey. Who are you again?"

Jax squared up to his full height. "I'm responsible for her safety, as you know."

Hailey stared up at them both. "It won't take long. Let me just do it."

"Val said I was to get you back to the hotel right away."

Her brows creased. "When did you talk to her?"

"I always talk to her. She gives me my daily briefings."

She looked surprised to hear this. "Can we wrap this up quickly?" she asked Abe. He left them to it, walking over to the side, not too far from her so that she was within his line of sight.

"When are you going to introduce us?" Patrick hissed, appearing out of nowhere.

"Sorry, dude. I will. I promise, I just can't do it now."

"What? Why not?"

"I can't, sorry."

"But she's right there." Patrick nodded his chin towards the table where Abe had made himself comfortable and the film crew were gathered around.

"She's right there. It won't take long."

"What's the rush, dude? Can't you see she's busy?" he snapped, unleashing the anger he felt for Abe onto his friend. Feeling bad, he apologized. "Sorry, dude. I'll figure something out. Another time, okay?"

"You just want her all to yourself," Patrick complained.

That made him laugh. "Do you see me having Hailey Ross all to myself?"

"You have the Midas touch," Patrick whined. "You get all the good things."

"Midas didn't get all the good things. He turned things to gold."

Patrick snorted. "And you being around Hailey Ross twenty-four seven isn't as good as turning things to gold?"

Despite this rush of new feelings, he was always acutely aware of the differences between them. She was nothing like the diva that he had at first thought. But in the real world, knowing who they were, there was no chance for anything to happen between them. "A woman like her, and someone like me, we've got nothing in common."

She raised her hand and swept back a stray lock of golden hair. He'd sometimes been tempted to do that himself. She motioned for him to come over. She needed him. "I can't believe you're not introducing her to me," he heard Patrick say before he rushed to her side, leaving Patrick talking to himself.

Hailey coughed. "Sorry, my throat's dry. Any chance you could get me some more water?" She lifted up her empty bottle.

"Back in a moment." He rushed back and asked Patrick to go and buy a couple of bottles, not wanting to turn his back to Hailey. His friend gave him a stony look. "It's not for me," Jax told him. "It's for Hailey. Please, I'll try to find another time for you both to meet."

Patrick stomped off only to return shortly with two bottles of water which Jax took over to her. Abe and his team appeared to have finished. He waited for Hailey to finish drinking from the bottle and then, when she had waved goodbye to the small number of fans now left in the mall, they got ready to leave.

She was quiet the entire way back and even on the elevator going up to their rooms.

He had to go in and check her hotel room. "Uh ..." he didn't want to alarm her, but he had to do as Val had instructed. "I need to check your hotel room."

Her eyes flashed. "Why?"

"Val asked me to."

"When?"

"Yesterday."

She stopped and faced him. "Is there something you're not telling me?"

"Nope." He wasn't going to tell her what he knew.

"Are you lying to me, Jackson?"

"No." It was a hard 'no'. He loved the way she called him Jackson when everyone else called him Jax. "It's a precaution. I swear I'm not asking you just because I want to get into your room." He tried to make light of the fact that he'd had to lie to her.

Hailey's cheeks blushed ever so slightly. The blush made him reconsider his words. "I'm only kidding. You know me."

"Do I?"

He paused with his hand reaching into his pocket for her key card, "You know me better now than you did before." He opened the door to her room. As much as he wanted to add to this conversation, time was of the essence. He motioned for her to stay where she was while he went inside the room and checked it out. Looking behind the curtains, and under the bed, and in the closets, he was satisfied that all was okay. "All fine," he said, walking towards her but she had already come inside and closed the door. "Didn't I tell you to stay outside?"

"And what if someone suspicious looking had approached me outside?" She stood in the middle of the room with her arms folded. "What then?"

"Good point." He scratched his chin. "I would have come running."

"Is there something you're not telling me?" she asked again.

"I know as much as you. It's probably just a precaution. The crowds are getting bigger. People know you're here. Even my friend Patrick is itching to meet you. I guess Val is making sure that you don't have any eager hotel staff wanting to get an autograph."

She sighed loudly, then sat on the couch, fell onto it more like. She looked exhausted and he wasn't surprised. It had been a long day for her. Filming part of the documentary earlier today and then having the event signing.

"Was he there tonight?" she asked, taking her shoes off and massaging her foot. "Your friend?"

Jax hovered near the door, not wanting to leave. "He was there. He was annoyed at me because I'd promised to introduce you to him."

"Why didn't you?"

"Because I had to get you out of there quickly."

"But he's your friend. You could have brought him over."

"And you are my responsibility." Something inside him swelled as he said the words, but this time, instead of it being awkward, the air was charged with anticipation. "I have to keep you safe."

"You do."

That brought a smile to his lips. He opened the door, ready to head to his own room even though the sight of her sitting on the couch, massaging her foot, called to him. There wasn't a thing he could do about it but leave. "Well, goodnight then."

"Goodnight."

He had almost closed the door behind him when he heard her shout out. "Don't go."

Had she said that, or were his ears and his mind playing games?

"Don't go."

He turned around to find her standing up, throwing her arms around herself as if she needed the protection. "I haven't eaten. It's been a long night. You haven't eaten either, right?"

"No."

"I'm getting room service. You were too, probably."

His insides started to do some sort of crazy dance. "I can't leave the hotel, so it's always room service."

"That's decided then. Why don't we order something here?"

It would be breaking the boundaries of his role. Encroaching. Traversing unchartered waters. She was a movie star, but most days, to him, she was just Hailey.

"I would like that."

CHAPTER 21

*S*he was lonely and hungry for company but it wasn't the company of fans she sought, or the film crew, nor did she want Abe's adulation and intrusion.

She wanted friends.

Like Claire.

Like Jackson.

More Jackson.

And now that she had asked him, he was coming over shortly. He said he needed to get out of his suit. She needed to get out of her heels and get into something more comfortable.

They had placed the food order before he left, and now, knowing that he would return soon enough, she rushed around, changing into her loungewear and tidying the main room. Putting magazines and her half-read scripts into neat piles and removing her bottles of nail polish and nail files. In LA, she would have called her favorite nail technician over, as well as her makeup artist, but she had had to do all of that herself this time.

When he knocked, she smoothed down her hair and opened the door.

"You're not supposed to open the door without asking who it is." Jackson walked in looking very different in his casual sweatpants and sweatshirt. It was neither biker boy nor smart business attire.

It was yet another look for this man who was almost chameleon-like in the many facets he had shown her.

They ate and talked, salad for her, and a burger and fries for him, which made her wonder how he managed to have such a lean and muscled body.

It's not like she hadn't noticed.

Lately, it was all she *could* notice.

In Jackson, she found something she couldn't define or know how to react to. He was raw, and earthy, and sexy, in a way that a lot of the men she met in Hollywood weren't.

When he swept his hands through his hair, pushing it back because it sometimes fell forward into his eyes, or when he smiled, even if only subtly, when the corners of his lips turned up —all of these things made her heart swell.

They sat on two separate couches and she had an easy view of him. Maybe it was because it was late, and she was exhausted, or maybe because she was now at ease around him, she didn't feel self-conscious or as if she needed to watch her words.

She would never have done this with Bruce or anyone else, but sitting with Jackson and eating in her room, it didn't feel strange at all.

"I couldn't help but overhear the conversation earlier on the way to the mall."

She picked at her salad, looking for the olives and flakes of tuna and tried to remember. "Oh, that."

"Was it a part you didn't get?" he asked, probing.

Of course he had heard. Of course he knew. He seemed to pick up on most things. "I had my heart set on a role. I really wanted it so badly. It was completely different than anything I've done so far."

"Nothing like the Monica Martins roles?"

She cringed with embarrassment. Of course, he had seen the posters of her in her skimpy jungle clothing—as if anyone going on an adventure in the jungle with explosives, and spiders and creepy crawlies, would ever go dressed like that.

Fantasy.

She was selling a fantasy and she no longer wanted to do the same old thing time and time again.

"Nothing like those," she replied.

"What did you have your heart set on?"

She told him about the schoolteacher role and how disappointed she had been. He listened and said all the right words. Comforting words, telling her that the perfect role would be there for her when the time was right.

Then he got up and took the empty plate from her, putting everything back on the serving cart. She watched in quiet amazement. "Do you always clean up after other people?"

"My mom taught me to clean up after myself."

She couldn't help but smile at that.

"Thanks for dinner," he said.

"You're welcome. Thanks for having it with me."

"Anytime."

She was falling into the bubble; a space that opened up around her whenever she was near him. It was filled with something soft, cushy, warm and velvety and now she found herself tumbling into it. This snatched moment of time with him, over dinner, just one to one, made her feel warm and fuzzy all over. And an air of despondency settled over her at the idea that he was leaving.

She was tempted to quip that his girlfriend must be happy but stopped before she made a fool of herself. She could feel it, and sense it, the fluttering in her belly that had started long before he had walked in. But what if he couldn't?

What if he wasn't interested?

What if he didn't feel what she did?

What if he already had a girlfriend?

"Don't forget to do the chain after I leave."

His sudden ratcheting up of security, the way he'd asked to sweep the room before she went in, and now him telling her to put the hotel chain on, confirmed to her that something was definitely up. "What did Val say to you?"

"Nothing."

"Don't lie to me, Jackson."

He ground his jaw. "You've received some letters from a fan. Val got jittery."

Saddo fanmail. She bet it was the same person.

He walked towards her and for a moment she thought he was going to put his arms on her arms, as if he wanted to reassure her. But he didn't. "There's nothing to worry about, Hailey. You're here, and I'm only in the next room."

She often thought about that, and he was right. With Jackson in the next room, there was nothing to worry about.

Abe hit her with something unexpected one day. "We've come almost to the end of your incredible journey, Hailey, but there's something we haven't talked about."

She raised an eyebrow, sensing something underhanded. "I'm sure we've covered everything."

"Talk to me about romance and heartbreak. You've had your fair share of both."

The air knocked clean out of her lungs, as if he'd punched her. Abe had dived right in.

She had clearly stated that questions about romance were off the cards, but he had done it again sneakily, and been clever about it; not asking her outright about whether she was dating—or not —as was the case. He'd left it open, thrown the bait and waited to see if she took it.

Well, she wasn't going to. She forced a smile, trying to buy some time, grappling for an answer to such a pervasive question. "Romance isn't easy," she said slowly.

"I imagine it isn't. You've had quite a rollercoaster ride with the men in your life."

She blinked and smiled sweetly. "But I'm not at liberty to discuss any of them, Abe, you know that." He was baiting her and it was on the tip of her tongue to put him right, but she knew this was a tactic to get her talking, and she wouldn't.

He smiled back, undeterred. "You and Ricky Moretti, also known as Big Rock, he and you were child TV stars on the same show. Tell us how your friendship has fared over the years. We keep hearing rumors."

Time froze.

She panicked for an answer.

She refused to entertain any talk of Big Rock and despised this unexpected low blow Abe was dealing. Val would have a conniption fit when she found out.

Or would she?

Maybe Val had given him the go ahead for this line of questioning, given her own recent failed attempts at persuading Hailey to go along with the fake romance ruse.

"Hailey? Is there something you care to share?" Abe's sick smile grated on her more than sharp, long nails scratching along a blackboard.

Someone coughed.

It was Jackson. She could tell from that one short sound in the distance.

"Rick and I have been friends from the beginning, and we are only friends. Nothing more, despite what the tabloids would have you believe."

Abe leaned forward, giving her a now-we're-getting-somewhere grin. "It's not the tabloids, Hailey. That clip from the awards ceremony went viral. You two have a certain chemistry which is hard to ignore. Why don't you spill all?"

She laughed and even though she couldn't see him, she could feel Jackson hanging onto her every word. Tiny sparks of electricity skittered along her body as if he were sitting next to her and waiting for her every answer.

"Oh, Abe," she flicked her hair and dazzled him with her thousand-watt smile. "Things go viral every second of every day." She leaned forward and placed her hand on his knee, looked at him as seductively as she could. Made him blush. "See how I'm looking at you now?" She squeezed his knee, even though her body recoiled in disgust. "Don't be surprised if this goes viral, Abe." She snatched her hand away.

"You're good. You're very good," he said, leaning back in his chair, wrapped in an air of subtle defeat.

She beamed at him, even though she felt anything but happy. "I'm an actress. What do you expect?" She could feel Jackson watching and listening, and it made her feel self-conscious. He knew more about her than she did about him. All she knew was that Roxy wasn't his girlfriend, and that he had a black belt in karate.

"I think we'll call it a wrap. Good work."

She got up and rushed off the stage, not even stopping to talk to anyone along the way. Not even stopping to see where Jackson was. She was so angry, for herself, for her privacy, for Big Rock. All she could think of was to pick up the phone and ask Val why Abe was probing into such personal matters. These things were a big no-no. She wasn't the type of celebrity who talked about her past romances or new ones.

There had never been a romance with Big Rock, and there never would be. The recent rumors and speculation had been hyped up because that was what Hollywood did best. It created fairy tales from the fragments of people's emotions.

It was no surprise when Jackson caught up with her, overtaking her so that he reached the car and opened the door for her.

"I told you, you don't need to do that unless it's a fancy affair."

"I figured you might need it today."

He closed the door as she settled back and dropped her head on the headrest. Her anger simmered beneath the surface of her skin. Jackson knew—just like he knew most of her moods now.

The interview today had been lousy, and this coming after the news that she hadn't gotten the greatly coveted part put her in a dark mood. The only good thing in the last twenty-four hours had been her and Jackson, talking and eating in her room.

Jackson was silent the entire way home and she was thankful for it. It comforted her that he was not only on guard, keeping her safe, but that he could read her moods and be there for her. He comforted her without him even knowing.

"You okay?" he asked when they got into the elevator.

She was too pent up with rage to speak.

"Hailey?" He touched her arm. The mere feel of his hand on her unraveled her.

"I'm not okay." She was done with putting up guards and pretending that everything was okay. She turned towards him. "He wasn't supposed to. We agreed."

"He went too far. He had no right to ask those questions." His green eyes bore into hers. "But you were great. You dealt with him."

"I made him blush."

"I noticed."

She felt a bit better, slightly uplifted. Only he could make her feel better after that horrible interview. The doors opened and they walked out. Jackson put his hand over hers as she was about to slide her key card into the slot. "I have to sweep the room first, remember."

She stepped back. Just before he pushed the door open, he asked, "Big Rock, he's the guy from the new superhero movie, isn't he?"

"Yes."

The air turned cold and prickly. She folded her arms. "He's just a friend."

"It's none of my business." His tone indicated that it was. She waited in the doorway as he swept her room, and wondered why he had asked her, why he didn't sound so happy. Her tired heart seemed to have a tiny burst of energy.

"All good. Safe to go in."

"Why did you ask about Big Rock?" She needed the truth, in words, not looks and casual touches.

"Why? Uh ..." he seemed to falter. "Because he's such a cool dude. I saw the movie he was in. It was brilliant. Those stunts he did. Amazing!" Jackson sounded like a fan, not a jealous friend and his reply irked her. He didn't seem to care. It was all about Big Rock. Her earlier sense of elation plummeted.

"Want to do something?" he asked suddenly. "Go to the beach, or have an ice cream? Get some fresh air?"

She felt as if she had started to fall down a dark, deep precipice but with one suggestion he had he had reached in and pulled her out. "Get some fresh air?" She could do with fresh air and the sea breeze. She didn't even need any of those things. Just her and Jackson. That would suffice.

"Be with nature," he said. "You love that stuff."

"*You* don't."

"I'm finding it more agreeable now."

His tender grin made her feel as if everything was sunny and bright again.

"I would like that very much."

CHAPTER 22

They walked silently to the beach. Hailey seemed preoccupied and deep in thought. He sensed her jittery mood and decided against asking her a million questions. Abe had already done enough damage. As far as he was concerned, if she wanted to tell him something, she would, in her own time. He liked that she could talk to him and confide in him, though Val probably wouldn't see it like that. She would say his job was to keep Hailey safe.

He would keep her safe, but he would also be someone she could fall back on. Following her around, he had come to see that her life was lonely. It didn't help that she was away from her home, and without her friends and support structure, but he'd heard enough from the interviews with Abe to gauge that even back in LA, life wasn't always plain sailing. It sounded like an endless round of interviews and publicity events. Filming was hard. Press intrusion was hard. Nothing about it sounded like fun to him.

He remained quiet, lost in his own thoughts, the earlier conversation about Big Rock, and the insinuations Abe had made didn't sit well with him. He'd looked the guy up on his cell phone as soon after and he turned out to be exactly who Jackson thought it might be—the guy from the big Hollywood movie that came out in the summer.

Hailey was interested in him?

He couldn't see the attraction; couldn't see her going for someone like that. The guy was too big, too butch. He was good looking, but he was refined, not rugged in the way an action hero should be. He was too polished. But she had mentioned that they had known one another for years. Maybe they had other history together. Maybe they had started out as friends and it had turned into something else.

The thought of it unsettled him in a way he didn't want to acknowledge or address. As much as he had come to enjoy spending time with her, *looking after her,* he reminded himself, it had to end. It was going to end. It couldn't really become anything more because of who she was, and who he was. Being around her these past few weeks had changed things.

The fuzziness had started maybe when they'd called a truce on the beach. Or maybe it had started when Val had held that three-way phone conference and Hailey had looked shocked. Maybe that was why he'd called her a diva, pushing her away in a bid to keep the distance between them.

He had an eye for pretty, and she was beautiful, like a delicate flower. And now he had started to care about her. Hard not to when his main role had been about her safety.

It was just as hard to forget last night, and how the two of them had laughed and talked over dinner as if it was the most natural thing in the world. As if it didn't matter that she was famous, and he was nothing more than a security guard.

Taking care of her would be the biggest and brightest thing on his resume. And for her, maybe this episode in her life would be nothing more than a speck on a silk scarf.

He didn't want to analyze things too much, not wanting to

face the fact that he couldn't hide from his feelings about her. Being with someone all day for weeks was bound to have some effect. It was normal for him to think about her.

But all the time? Even when she wasn't with him?

It was normal, he told himself. It was all in the name of her safety and protection.

She wrapped her arms around herself, shivering. This close to the beach, the sea air was chilly. "You're cold." He stopped walking and turned to face her. "You should have gone in and grabbed a sweatshirt or jacket, or something. I thought you were going to go in and freshen up first."

She laughed. "Freshen up?"

"I heard you say that a few times." When the makeup artists were retouching her makeup. Sometimes she'd said that to Val on the phone.

"Freshen up my makeup," she cried, obviously finding his comment funny. She rubbed her arms and stared back at him.

"You don't need makeup. You definitely don't need to plaster more on."

Her eyes twinkled with amusement. "Is that what you think I do? Plaster my makeup on?"

A smile stretched across his face. "By the bucket load."

"Then you can see why I needed to freshen up all the time. I had to plaster more of it on."

"Yeah, I can see that. You needed to hide the witchy warts."

She roared with laughter. He could stare at her face for a hundred years and never get bored. "You're cold." He took the plunge and placed his hands on her arms then rubbed gently.

She gave him a peculiar look. Nothing to make him stop, though. "I'll be okay once we get walking."

"Look at these golf ball-sized goosebumps." He continued rubbing her arms, his boldness having been rewarded because she hadn't yet told him to stop.

She laughed at that. "Golf ball-sized?" He wanted to hug her to him, have her against his chest so that he could blanket her with his arms, and use all of his body heat to make her warm again. But that was an idle daydream. Taking off his jacket, he placed it over her shoulders, resisting the urge to reel her towards him and hug her.

"But you'll get cold," she protested.

"I've got a shirt on. Your arms are bare."

"Are you sure?"

"I can't have you freeze to death."

"Thank you."

They continued walking. "Better?" he asked her after a while.

"Better."

"Come on. Let's get some ice cream." But as he started to lead her towards the ice cream parlor, he noticed a large group of tourists hovering in front of it. He spun her around, grabbed her hand and started walking in the opposite direction.

"Hey!" she cried, squeezing his hand. "What's wrong?"

"We can't go there. There's a huge crowd of people outside. They'll recognize you the minute they see you."

"I'll hover around here on the beach, and you can go buy the ice cream," she suggested.

"No way. I'm not taking my eyes off you."

"In another universe that would sound sexy. I mean, endearing," she said quickly. "It would be endearing."

"In another universe I would hope you'd go with sexy."

They were still holding hands, only now she had stopped walking, so that he was forced to stop and face her.

"What did you say?" Her voice was soft, almost a whisper.

What was he supposed to do now? Tell her the truth? If she only knew that he hadn't slept much lately. He'd tossed and turned in bed these past few nights because all he could see when he closed his eyes was her. His mind would run through the things she had said or done during the day. This sustained him.

"I think you're cute," he answered, finally.

"Cute?" she didn't seem to like that, and moved her hand away.

"Yeah. Cute." He scratched his nose. "I have other words …"

"Words like?"

Words like sexy, and kind, and fun, and adorable, serious, and everything else on his checklist for what he wanted in a partner. Hailey Ross was all of those things. And more. She was looking at him intently, making him even more conscious of crossing the line. "I've got a better plan."

"I'll defer to your plan."

He walked quickly, not sure if it would still be open. There was a bookshop around here, and it had a coffee shop, and lots of nooks and crannies for her to hide in if the need arose.

"Books and Buns?" Hailey cried. "I love the name."

"You'll love it even more inside."

"Is it a coffee shop?" she asked.

"Coffee, hot drinks and they do lots of nice cakes, too." Women always liked cake. And chocolate. He figured he couldn't go too wrong.

"And cake, too," she purred. "Cake beats ice cream in my books."

"Now that's something I didn't know about you."

"You must know a whole lot of stuff about me. My life is an open book."

He didn't answer that but pulled the door open and let her go in first. The scent of warm baked cakes and coffee permeated the air. They found a table easily and he was pleased to see that the shop was relatively quiet. He glanced at his watch. They could while away a few hours here.

Hailey pulled her baseball cap down low to avoid getting attention. She stuck her face into a magazine when the server came over, and since she had already told him what she wanted—coffee and a slice of cherry cake—he ordered for the both of them.

When the cake came, she sighed with contentment as she took a forkful. He had ordered black coffee only. No dessert.

"No cake?" she asked in shock.

He shook his head.

"Is that because you're counting calories?"

He patted his stomach. "I have to watch my figure." He faked a woman's accent, and badly.

"Your figure?" she asked. "I know what that's like, but I don't care about that now."

"I'm glad you don't."

"I'm on vacation. Want to try some?" she asked. "Because I feel like a pig eating all of this." It was a huge serving of cake.

"No thanks. You go ahead. You're the one who's had a tough day."

She lifted another forkful to her mouth, and he liked that she was enjoying the cake and coffee. "Tough doesn't even begin to cut it. I should never have agreed to this documentary."

"Why did you?" He didn't understand why people did things they didn't want to do.

"It's part and parcel of what I do. You make a movie; you have to get publicity. My career is starting to plateau, so I need all the publicity I can get. Doing this documentary is supposed to help."

She didn't sound happy about it; she didn't look happy. He wanted to reach out and take her hand, tell her it would be okay, but he couldn't. "Things will pick up," was all he could say.

"If I don't change things up soon, I'll be destined to be forever cast in the role of an action heroine who should really know how to dress for the jungle." This got a laugh from him, but it was no laughing matter for her. "I'll always be known as this action woman deep in the jungles of Ecuador."

"You have a lifetime ahead of you, Hailey. This isn't the end. A couple of rejections don't define you."

"I'm sorry. This sounds like a first world problem. Woe is me, sitting here with all the money and fame in the world. I know this must sound silly to you."

"Why, because I'm just a security guard?"

"Why do you always say that?"

He pressed his lips together. "Sorry." Over her shoulder, he could see a couple of women a few tables away kept looking her way. He hoped they would leave her in peace to enjoy some time to herself.

"You think that people see you a certain way, but they don't."

He held her gaze, needing her to tell him how she saw him, but she remained silent. He was getting complacent and losing sight of the boundary line between his job and who she was to him. If he wasn't careful, he was going to end up making a fool of himself, pining for her long after she left him and Starling Bay in her rearview mirror. He shrugged.

"They don't, Jackson. I don't."

"No?" The hope inside him started to lift, tiny little baby wings learning to take flight. He waited patiently, hoping she would elaborate, but a group of ladies from the other table had come over and rudely interrupted them. Not outright, but they hovered a little distance away, and it was enough for her to notice them.

"Oh, boy. Can't they leave you alone?" he grumbled.

"It's okay. Most people here have been pretty good."

He huffed out an angry breath. Only Hailey would think that

this was okay. It wasn't. They had been in the middle of a conversation, skirting around the flimsy and fragile edges of the friendship that was springing between them. Instead, he had to watch Hailey sign autographs and take pictures with people she didn't know and would likely never meet again.

CHAPTER 23

She had loved spending that time with only the two of them sitting in the coffee shop and talking. She wanted more times like that.

It was no longer enough just to be near Jackson in the car, or as she walked along, and he cleared the way for her. That wasn't conducive to them having a decent conversation. She wanted to sit with him and talk.

To just be.

Jackson didn't pry, or probe, or need anything from her. He listened, he supported, he cared. She *needed* this.

With Jackson, it was different.

He didn't care who she was.

He listened and gave advice and then he would tell her about himself. It was an exchange, of words and thoughts and feelings.

The next few days of filming the documentary passed by without any major problems and she woke up on Saturday morning feeling happier than she had in days because it meant that she had the weekend to herself.

No Abe, no film crew, no reason to get all made up and dressed.

She suddenly longed to go back to the lake. With Jackson.

The idea made her jump out of bed, shower and get ready. Except that she didn't bother with the makeup. Not even a touch of mascara. For once, she felt as if she didn't need to put on her Hailey face. She texted Jackson.

Hailey: How about we go to the lake?

Jackson: Sounds good. When?

Hailey: Now?

Jackson: I'll get ready.

As she was ready, she went over and knocked on his door. But when he opened it, she couldn't help but stare at his arms, at the muscles peeking out from his sleeves. At the tattoos which she could only see a part of.

His hair was wet, damp more than sopping wet, and he looked clean and fresh, and smelling like sea breeze and mint.

She managed to open her mouth and make it work. "You said you were ready."

He shot her an amused look. "I said I was *getting* ready, besides, who told you to come out of your room and walk over to mine?"

"I—uh … uh …" what had happened to her elocution lessons? All the work with the voice coaches to ensure she could speak and enunciate well seemed to vanish when she was around this man.

She prided herself on being calm and confident, yet Jackson Miller could easily turn her into a stuttering wreck. "I can come back later, when your hair is dry."

"It'll dry quickly. It always does."

"You'll catch a cold."

"You can keep me warm," he told her.

Was he flirting with her? She felt the color rise to her cheeks. She hovered in the doorway while he quickly got his things together and then they left, heading into the elevator. Neither of them spoke and when she looked at him he was staring ahead as the elevator doors opened.

She followed him to the parking lot, to where he'd left his bike, and then, with helmets on, they got on. She sat behind him, hugging him, holding onto him and they were at the lake less than an hour later. Like last time, they left the bike in the parking lot near the row of stores again, then walked through the woods towards the lake. This time Jackson suggested they try a different route, taking the longer way around.

She was happy that he had made this suggestion, and she told him so. "This is nice, going this way around."

"Yeah?" The ground was uneven, and trees crowded together making it almost impossible to see the sky through the thickness of their branches. They soon came to a little stream. Jackson made a calculated leap and landed on the other side. He held out his hand for her to take in case she fell.

"I can make the jump," she said, resisting. She surveyed the way the bank slanted, knowing she could easily cross the stream, but she needed to have a firm footing on the bank when she landed on the other side. Maybe it would have made sense to take up the offer of his supporting arm.

He placed his hands on his hips and watched. "You sure? I wouldn't want you to fall and break a leg. Val would fire me at once. I can already imagine the headlines: *Hollywood Star Falls in Bodyguard's Care*."

She laughed. "You say the craziest things."

"It could happen." He held his hand out again, and once more she refused to take it. She could do this. "I'm not a diva. Only a diva would take your hand."

"A diva would want me to carry her in my arms. I can do that, if you want?" He raised a sexy eyebrow.

She tried to stifle a giggle. "I'm not a diva."

"No."

"I'm not a Hollywood superstar. That's not how I see myself. That's not how I want you to see me."

His brow wrinkled as she pushed the boundaries of what and who they were. "What do you want me to see you as?" he echoed, uncertainty bubbling in his voice.

The silence swelled and rose, like a souffle. She waited for it to deflate. She was prying, scraping, pushing the boundaries of what they were to one another. Could she take the risk? Perhaps it was better to stay guarded, to hide what she really felt in her heart.

"As a normal person."

He quirked a brow at her. "You are a normal person."

If she wasn't careful, she was going to do something silly, like land in the stream, or lose her balance when crossing to the other side. Or feel herself falling into his big, strong arms. The way he was looking at her, she knew he would not let her fall.

She decided to jump without his help. The breadth of the divide wasn't too wide. She leapt and landed by his side. "Wasn't too difficult at all." She clapped her hands together feeling thankful that she hadn't fallen flat on her face given how much her heart was beating.

They set off walking again.

"You're good at almost everything," he told her.

"How would you know?"

"Because I'm slowly watching all of your movies."

"All of them?" she asked faintly.

"All of them, starting from the oldest ones and working my way up."

"Why?" The heat rose and warmed her cheeks as she remembered how bad she had been in some of the earlier movies.

"Why not? It's not every day I get to be a bodyguard to Hollywood royalty."

She stopped walking. "Please stop saying that."

He stopped walking as well. "I'm sorry."

"I'm not a diva."

"You're not."

"I'm not a Hollywood superstar."

He made a face as if he didn't agree. "Technically … okay, you're not."

"I'm not Hollywood royalty."

He winced. "Again … okay, you're not."

"I'm just Hailey."

He nodded. "You're just Hailey." His voice turned gravelly and low, so low that she could hear the reverberations in her stomach.

Or were they butterflies?

He raised his hand and cupped the side of her face. Everything around her ground to slow motion as the warmth of his hand seeped through to her skin. Her insides grew hot, hot, hotter, and she lost sight of her surroundings. The world around her consisted just of him and her. He lowered his head just as she tilted her face towards him. His lips brushed lightly against hers. But a loud rustling erupted out of nowhere. They sprang apart. Something huge charged towards them. Hailey screamed, as Jackson pushed her behind him.

"Spart! Stay!"

It was that dog again.

In the next second, the dog's owners appeared as Hailey came out from behind Jackson.

"Spart!" Dylan admonished.

"Did he scare you?" Merry asked. "I'm so sorry if he did."

"He just caught us off guard," Hailey replied. Her heart was beating as if it was going to explode inside her chest. But it wasn't from being caught off-guard. Nor was it anything to do with the huge dog. Her lips tingled from the imprint of Jackson's light kiss.

The man put the beast back on the lead and the couple walked over to them. "We meet again. Merry, Dylan," said the man, waving a hand between them. "I hope he didn't scare you."

"It's okay," said Jackson, shaking the man's hand. "You're Reed's friend, aren't you?"

"That's right. Do you know him?"

"I know Reed and Rourke," Jackson explained. "You looked familiar. I'm sure we've met in passing."

Dylan grinned at them while the dog strained at the leash again. "It's a small world."

"It sure is."

They parted ways because the dog was raring to take off, seeing the tempting woods before him.

"That is one big dog," said Jackson.

"He must eat a lot," she remarked, and wondered if he was going to mention what had taken place before they had been interrupted. They had crossed a line now. She hadn't imagined it.

"We should head back," Jackson suggested.

"Oh, okay." Didn't seem as if he was going to mention it.

CHAPTER 24

It was early evening by the time they returned to the hotel and went to their separate rooms. They'd been out for hours although it hadn't seemed like hours.

She was ravenous.

Jackson must be too.

She knocked on his door, one arm folded against her chest while she wondered what she was doing. He still hadn't said anything about the almost-kiss. Neither had she, but they couldn't pretend it hadn't happened.

He opened the door quickly, his eyes scanning around the hallway behind her, almost as if she'd come to him because something was wrong. "Everything okay?"

He was acting normal, and she was determined to do the same. "Do you want to eat? I was going to get takeout. You must be starving."

His mouth fell open. "I …"

"We've eaten together before, Jackson. It's no big deal."

He gave her pointed stare and for a moment she thought he was going to broach the subject. That huge, big, hulking elephant-sized subject of their almost-kiss. "Burgers and fries?" he said.

Her insides sank, but she regained her composure just as quickly. "Same as last time? Sure. Come over in fifteen. It should be here by then."

He showed up well before the food arrived, telling her it would be good so that he could check that it was room service and no one else.

"Who else would it be?"

He didn't answer, but gave her that knowing, million-megawatt smile that she had found cheesy at first, as if it were the type of smile he tried on with most women.

Suddenly, she didn't want him to have a smile for any woman but her. It was an odd thought, coming as it did out of nowhere. She would think about it later. She would analyze everything in detail; what was happening, what they weren't talking about, what they were skirting around.

They sat opposite one another at the dining table, surveying the dome-shaped platters that lay before them. Hailey lifted the lid to one. "Hmmmm."

He lifted the lid to another one. "Tasty." It was almost like an amusing game. Not because there was going to be any huge surprise, after all they had ordered this, but because it was fun. And because they were both starving, they ate well and plentifully.

He made her laugh, telling her about some of the interesting things he'd witnessed doing his odd security jobs, both in the malls and other venues, and in the specialized jobs he'd done for Reed and his friends.

Later, when they were finished, they both put everything back neatly on the serving tray.

"I hate leaving a mess for others to clean up," she said.

"Wish more people thought that way, especially at the mall. Some of those tables at the food court can get really messy."

She didn't want him to leave once dinner was over. She didn't like the idea of sitting in her hotel room alone, watching TV or trying to read something. "Did you want to watch some TV?" she suggested as he hovered around the table, and she sat on the couch.

"Watch some TV?"

Maybe he had plans. "Unless you've got somewhere to be."

He chortled. "I can't be anywhere where you aren't. I have to have my eyes on you the whole time."

She sat up, trying to gauge his tone, his mood. Did he want to be somewhere else instead? "I won't go anywhere, I promise, if you have plans. You can go. I'll lock myself inside."

His eyebrows lifted. "I don't have other plans. I don't want to be anywhere else."

"Really?" Things suddenly seemed brighter.

"I like being here with you."

He couldn't have made her any happier. "Really?"

"Are you sure you want me to watch TV with you?"

For a big, tall, muscular guy with tats, he was being pretty hesitant about his moves. "I wouldn't have asked if I didn't want you to."

He slowly shifted onto the couch, as if he wasn't sure. As if having eaten a meal together didn't automatically entitle him to spending time with her.

"Why are you so freaked out, Jackson?"

"Because what we do … what we did … can change things."

Her smile faded. "Would that be such a bad thing?"

"I don't want to go stepping on any toes."

"Stepping on toes?" she asked, needing clarification, wanting to know his thoughts.

"You and Big Rock and all …"

She gazed up at the ceiling. "I told you we're just friends."

He scratched behind his ear and sniffed. "What if he showed up right now at your door? What would he think?"

That's what he was worried about? She didn't know what to tell him, and at the same time the idea that he was concerned about her and Big Rock somehow made her hopeful.

"He would be fine about it." He wouldn't think anything of it. She and Big Rock both wanted the same thing—and a Hollywood-style arranged romance or marriage wasn't part of it. They had a mutual respect and understanding, and she wasn't going to tell Jackson about him, even though she felt certain he could keep a secret. This secret was not hers to give away. She was a good friend like that, and she wasn't about to abuse Big Rock's trust.

"He'd be fine? With you and me sitting here, hanging out like this?"

"It's not like we're doing anything," she pointed out, twisting her body so that she was facing him, trying to curb the yearning inside her.

"No, we're not."

Say it, she urged. *Say what you mean.* It had to come from Jackson first, she didn't want to take the lead and expose her feelings towards him. From what he was saying, it sounded as if he cared, but she didn't want subtext. She wanted him to say it out loud. She wanted him to say what had happened in the woods. "Is there something you want to—"

"That damn dog. He has such bad timing." He twisted to the side so that they were almost facing one another.

Her heart skipped a few beats. "Such bad timing," she agreed. Jackson shifted closer. She leaned forward. He lifted his hand and gently caressed her face. Her insides went all wobbly. He licked his lips. She tilted her head, her lips parted. And the sound of her cell phone's ringtone jolted her.

Jackson sprang back. The moment iced and crashed. She stared at the phone, her body a mess of shock and disappointment.

"You should get that," he murmured softly.

She snatched the phone, the caller display telling her that it was Val. "I've found the perfect dress for the premiere."

It took a few seconds for the words to make sense. Jackson's eyes on her, made her skin go all tingly. She could smell his aftershave. Could not forget the feel of his hand against her skin. "The dress. Oh, okay," she said, her voice sounding oddly bland. She didn't care for the dress, or the premiere.

"It's Dior," said Val excitedly.

Hailey glanced at Jackson, who stared back helplessly. Val wittered on, the words gushing out of her at breakneck speed, but Hailey didn't care. She wasn't interested. It made her wish she hadn't answered the call.

"What's wrong? Why aren't you getting excited?"

Jackson raised an eyebrow, then sat forward, as if he were getting all antsy.

Hailey turned her back to him. "Can I talk to you later?"

"Why? Where are you?"

"I'm busy." It was the wrong thing to say. Val was nosy and would want specifics. With Jackson listening, she couldn't very well get out of it.

"I'm in my hotel room. We're watching TV."

"We? Who's *we?*"

She swallowed. That was one detail she should have left out. "Jackson."

"What?" Val shrieked. Hailey's insides hollowed out. "Your *bodyguard?*"

She stood up and walked away, certain that Jackson had heard Val.

"Yes," she hissed under her breath.

"Why are you watching TV with your *bodyguard?*"

"It's been a long day, can you leave it, please?"

"But your *bodyguard?*" Val echoed.

She turned around, her cheeks burning, her heart dipping as

she saw Jackson get up and head towards the door. He made a yawning motion, and put his hands together, indicating that he was going to bed.

Then he left.

She turned to Val and snapped. "We had something to eat. It was late. What's the big deal?"

"This isn't like you, Hailey. What's going on?"

"Nothing is going on."

"About the dress, it's black, just the color you—"

She didn't care about the dress. She didn't care about the movie premiere. She didn't care about Val, or Big Rock, or her movie.

She cared about Jackson and the opportunity that had been snatched away again. "Call me tomorrow. I have a headache." She hung up and stared at the empty room, the empty couch, and lamented about the empty wasted evening this had turned into.

CHAPTER 25

Maybe this was a sign. Twice today he'd almost kissed her, and twice they had been interrupted.

Surely this was a sign for him to stay away? What had he been thinking, almost about to kiss Hailey Ross, *the* Hailey Ross? He walked into his suite and closed the door behind him. Brushing his hands across his hair he wondered how the heck he'd lost control.

It hadn't been only his doing.

He knew his place, but with Hailey, he sometimes forgot who he was, who she was. He didn't believe that anyone was better than him, or vice versa. Like not getting involved with someone who was so far out of his orbit that once the initial attraction had passed, he was sure they would have nothing in common.

Even as he tried to force this belief on himself, it wasn't true. Hailey was as down to earth and as agreeable as any decent woman he knew. She had a heart of gold and a caring side that most people probably didn't think she possessed. They saw only the glamor.

And equally, there were also certain boundaries that had to be respected, especially given that this was a job. This was work. He had no excuse for messing up. This wasn't a case of him casually walking up to someone in a bar and hitting on her.

He had tried to keep his distance, but it had been Hailey who had asked him to come over so that they could eat.

Who was he kidding? He crashed onto the couch, sighing. He lay with his arms behind his head, staring up at the ceiling and wondering how the heck he was going to keep away from her.

Nothing could come of this.

Nothing.

Sure, his heart leapt for joy each time he saw her and each day was full of good things. Just being around her was enough. It was almost like dating, without all that complicated stuff.

But he wanted more and he could see that she did, too. But she was going to break his heart and leave, then never come back. He would have to bear seeing her on the silver screen with all the hottest guys, and he'd have to learn to deal with it.

The walls of his room were closing in. He wanted to get on his bike and go for a long ride. Maybe clear his head a little.

Figure out where he was at.

Figure out what he was going to do when Hailey returned to LA.

Figure out how he was going to bury the memories and imprints of her that had become embedded in his heart.

He hadn't expected to feel this way about her; about the diva movie star who was anything but that.

His cell phone buzzed in his pocket, his spirits soared. Hailey had decided to go somewhere. He pulled it out quickly, anticipating the sound of her voice.

"Where are you?" It was Roxy. He almost groaned out loud, but thankfully he stopped himself in time. His sister wouldn't have appreciated it.

"I'm … working," he replied, being evasive.

"I haven't seen you in weeks."

"I've *been* working."

"Don't you get any time off?"

"Not really."

"That's not right. You're watching over Hailey Ross and you don't get time off? Aren't there supposed to be two of you doing shifts?"

"It's not a big deal."

"It is when my little bro is being worked to death."

He grunted in irritation. "I'm not being worked to death."

"I'm coming over."

"No, Rox, don't." But she had already hung up.

She showed up not so long after. "What's this?" he asked, when she carefully set down a large bag on the coffee table.

"Some of your favorite dishes."

"I'm not starving to death."

"I should hope not." His sister took off her jacket and cast her eyes around the room. "Nice."

"It's not bad." He sniffed and folded his arms as Roxy surveyed the entire suite, sneaking a look into the bedroom and the bathroom. "Very, very nice."

"Thanks."

"Aren't you going to be civil? Offer me a cold drink at least?" She made herself at home on the couch which meant she was staying for a while. Probably wanting to hear some gossip.

"Uh…yeah, sure." He got a can of iced tea from the fridge, pulled the pull tab back and handed it to her. "That's all I have." Why was she here? She had never been particularly interested in what he did before. But then he'd never had a job that was like this before.

She took a sip. "So, what's she really like, this Hailey Ross."

"What do you have against her?" He was most curious to know. "Are you jealous?"

"Oh, puh-leese." Roxy wrinkled her nose. "Jealous of what?"

"I have no idea, because you don't even know her, so it can't be that, but then again, I don't know how female minds work."

"Jealous? Of Hailey Ross?" Roxy sneered.

His sister could be opinionated, and feisty. A fireball at times, so he wouldn't be surprised if this was the case. Women could be catty, and he was certain that Hailey had her fair share of haters as well as the crazies who probably professed their undying love for her.

"I don't *hate* her. I just don't like the idea of celebrity."

"You don't like the *idea* of celebrity?" he chortled. "What's that got to do with anything? Hailey's from this town, she went to our school. I get that you're not remotely interested in her, but to be catty all the time doesn't make sense."

"It doesn't seem fair. I'm busy working all the hours, all the days, and she swans into town looking all glam, and with a bodyguard, and an entourage—"

"Hailey doesn't like security detail. She has no entourage. She's low-key."

"Jax." Roxy blinked. "You. Are. Smitten." She cupped her face and gave him a tell-me-more look. "Are you?"

"What?" he chortled. "Don't be silly."

"You are."

"Shhh."

Roxy's eyes twinkled with surprise. Trust Roxy to pick up on it. "That's the stupidest thing I've heard." A knock at the door saved him. He rushed to open it but his heart almost shocked right out of his chest when he found Hailey staring back at him.

"What's the stupidest thing you've ever heard?"

"What?" Now he was stuck. The idea of Roxy and Hailey meeting gave him a rash.

"Hey," she swatted his arm playfully as she walked past him and into the suite. "Oh, sorry, I didn't realize Jackson had company," he heard her say.

He turned around to find Hailey and Roxy staring at one another. It was almost like a standoff.

Roxy held out her hand. "I'm Jax's sister, Roxy."

Hailey shook her hand. "We were at your diner a few weeks ago."

"I know. I remember. I should have come over and said 'hi', but I figured you probably get noticed all the time and you get disturbed a lot so ..."

"It's nice to meet you, finally." Hailey was being gracious. "What's the stupidest thing you've heard?" she asked again, putting him in a tight spot. He could feel the heat of Roxy's penetrating glare. She was reading the room, and him and Hailey, and drawing her own conclusions.

He was going to have to deal with a thousand questions after this.

"Rox was saying something about one of her customers. It's not that funny." He wondered why Hailey had come over. And he also wished that Roxy hadn't come at all. An awkward silence filled the space, growing and swelling by the second.

"Did you, uh... would you like something to drink?" Roxy asked, turning extra friendly as she smiled sweetly at Hailey.

"No, thanks. We just ate, uh ..." She looked at him and clasped her hands together, as if she didn't know what to do with them, or what to say.

"*You* just ate?" Roxy waved her hand at them both. She didn't miss a thing.

Hailey looked at him. "Uh ... I wanted to say, uh, that was Val who called."

"Sure." He cleared his throat. "Yeah. I spoke to her earlier." He hadn't, but whatever this ruse was that Hailey was continuing with, it was better for him to go along.

"She said, uh, that details for the uh ... premiere were fine."

Jackson coughed. "Cool. Thanks for that." He strode towards

the door, feeling Roxy's death stare on his back. His sister's questions would come at him like a firing squad once Hailey left.

"Don't go!" Roxy cried. "Jax, will you stop being so rude and ask Hailey to come in?"

"Hailey was leaving. She has a busy schedule tomorrow." He opened the door and indicated for Hailey to leave. Having these two women together was a big hell no.

"I should go," Hailey said.

"Okay, bye." The look of pain in her eyes cut right through him, but having these two together in one room was not a good idea.

Roxy rushed over to the door. "I was wondering," she said to Hailey. "How do we get tickets to the movie premiere?"

"You want to come?"

"Yes, we want to come! It's going to be a big event, big for Starling Bay."

"I'm not sure how it's being promoted here—"

"I'm sure Hailey can find out later and let me know, and then I'll let you know." He was eager to close the door before Roxy imposed herself and invited herself to Hailey's suite.

Hailey looked hurt and confused. "I'll … I'll try to find out for you."

"Thank you," Roxy said. He bit down on his jaw, ashamed by the display of his sister's two-facedness.

Even as she nodded, Hailey's eyes drifted away from him, her A-lister guard switched on as well as an easy smile. It only made him feel even more ashamed. This was for the best. "Okay then. Goodnight," he said.

"Bye."

"It was nice to meet you," Roxy said, flashing Hailey a smile so plastic that it made him wish he was an only child. "It's a shame you couldn't stay."

He closed the door, knowing that her last comment was for his benefit. His sister grinned at him like a fool. "You have the hots for that girl."

"How two-faced were you?" He rubbed his forehead.

"What's that all about, Jax? And *Jackson*? She calls you *Jackson*. See what I mean about her having airs?"

"She has airs because she calls me Jackson?" he snapped. "How old are you? Three?" He hated the way he'd reacted just now in front of Hailey. He didn't want Roxy to be in on anything, because she would tease him mercilessly but the truth of it was that they had almost kissed. It was a huge deal. He hadn't even had time to process it when she'd turned up.

"You can't go there, Jax." Roxy's face turned serious. "You can't, you hear me?"

"I don't know what you're talking about."

"I know you, little bro. I know what you're like when you get all dreamy-eyed over someone."

"You're delirious."

"You like her, and I can tell, she likes you too."

"You're hilarious." He moved away and picked up the TV remote, then turned the TV on, pretending he wasn't paying attention to anything she said.

"You always did have an eye for a pretty woman, but Hailey Ross is bad news. She's not interested in you, you do realize that, don't you?" Roxy stood in front of the TV, blocking his view.

"I am not interested in her," he growled.

Roxy pursed her lips together. "You better not be. That woman is bored and lonely. She doesn't have any friends and no one to talk to but you."

"Thanks. You're making me feel really good."

"I'm not insulting you, little bro, it's her. She's the problem. Don't go falling for her looks."

"You should go."

Roxy shook her head slowly, a line appearing between her

brows. "It's worse than I thought. You're in love with her." She snatched her coat from the couch. "I thought you'd know better, Jax. She's so far out of your league, you're going to end up making an idiot of yourself."

She slammed the door on her way out.

Tough love. That was what Roxy was giving him. It was good advice. He ought to take it, because she was right.

She was so right.

CHAPTER 26

*H*e had cold-shouldered her, and she didn't understand why.

Jackson was being odd. She had suspected a coldness in his attitude towards her when his sister was over. In the way he'd tried to shoo her out of his room, as if he couldn't get her out fast enough, as if they hadn't spent all day walking through the woods, talking and getting to know one another, as if they hadn't come back and had dinner in her room, as if they hadn't almost kissed.

As if it had all been a dream.

She had detected a chill between them that very moment, and the next day she waited for a text or a sign, a knock on the door, *something*.

But there had been nothing. She had stayed in on Sunday, and done absolutely nothing.

For the first time ever, she didn't mind Abe's questions. She was glad to have the distraction, of having something else to focus on during those awkward silences with Jackson. Neither of them had spoken much on the way down the elevator or during the car ride.

Had he been upset by what Val had said? There was no mistaking the fact that he'd heard her. Even when she had later gone over to apologize to him, when his sister had shown up, she'd had the distinct and unshakeable feeling that they had been talking about her.

He'd behaved oddly, and he had never answered her question even though she had asked him twice about what was the stupidest thing he'd heard?

They had been talking about her, and now she wondered if they had been laughing about her behind her back as well.

After those wonderful days with Jackson, him now being so distant and cold made her feel more alone than ever.

Desperate for female company, she arranged to meet Claire. She needed to talk to someone she could trust, even though she wasn't sure she had anything worth confiding in Claire about.

Had it been real, these feelings between her and Jackson? Or did he see her as a quick way to have some fun? Would she ever know?

She had considered asking Claire to come to the hotel, which meant Jackson wouldn't be hovering around with his supersonic hearing, but guilt poured over her at the idea that she was using Claire as a sounding board. Wanting to do something nice for her friend, she made a reservation at Fellini's, an amazing restaurant that she and her family had only gone to on very special occasions. She booked two tables, one for Jackson a couple of tables away.

"Are you sure about this, Hales?" Claire sat across from her, gawking at the decor and the interior. "I've never been here before."

Hailey smiled, feeling good that she had decided they come here. Over her friend's shoulder, she caught sight of Jackson. Their gazes met and held, before she forced herself to look away.

He wasn't near enough to hear, which made her feel relieved. She didn't want Jax's bat-like hearing to pick up on anything.

Not wanting to dive into her own drama, they ordered their food first and then she let Claire do most of the talking, about her children and her life and what she was up to, but with Claire it was all about the children. Hailey loved listening about them, but it quickly became evident that it was her children that made up most of Claire's day and her life.

It made her wonder if she could give up her career to take a break.

For a family.

For a husband.

It was something she hadn't thought much about.

Future and long-term wasn't something that was on her radar. She only thought short-term stuff: the roles she was going to audition for, the scripts she had been reading, the premiere next week, the documentary and how it would be received.

She listened while Claire regaled her with stories about what the kids had been up to. There had been a funny episode last week when Claire had cut vegetables-including onions and mushrooms for a casserole, and sliced apples ready to make an apple pie. Freddie watched Cicely take a bite of apple, and then she would hand him a piece of onion and the poor boy wouldn't realize what had happened. Hailey doubled over in laughter and laughed so hard that she accidentally knocked over a glass of water.

"I'm so clumsy sometimes," she wailed, feeling foolish as she tried to mop up the water that was leaking out onto the white silk tablecloth. She knew Jackson would have seen it.

"Here." Claire had pulled out a huge pile of tissues from her handbag to mop up the liquid. "Always be prepared," she explained. "With the children, you'd be surprised how much I have to carry."

Servers swarmed their table and within a few moments, had

lifted the entire contents of the table, from the centrepiece decked with orchids and candles, to their plates, glasses and silverware. They changed the tablecloth within seconds while the restaurant owner who had come over first and fussed over them chatted to Hailey. She was eager to get back to her conversation with Claire.

Their food arrived shortly, and they ate, discussing TV shows and movies with Claire asking her about actors she had met.

She wanted gossip, of which Hailey had plenty. It was a good conversation, and it took her mind off things, until she looked up and saw Jackson sitting at his table alone, on his cell phone. Unlike the last time, their gazes didn't meet so much. He didn't stare her way, and she was starting to think that the blissful days they had spent together had been fleeting.

"He's so cute," Claire sighed, looking over her shoulder. Claire waved back when Jackson lifted his hand to catch a server's attention.

What if it were just the two of them, her and Jackson, sitting here together having a meal?

Val would be shocked. Would the world also be shocked?

Maybe it was time she stopped caring what the world thought and went along with what her heart wanted.

The problem was Jackson didn't want this. They had started to become closer—or so she had thought— maybe he'd *thought* he'd wanted her, but maybe he was glad now they hadn't kissed.

"What do you two talk about?" Claire asked excitedly. "You have all that time together. He follows you around all day, doesn't he?"

"He's always around, but we don't talk much."

"I don't believe that!"

If Claire had asked her last week, Hailey might have had something different to tell her, about how much closer she and Jackson were becoming. "It's purely professional."

Claire leaned towards her. "He's gorgeous. How do you manage to keep your hands off him?"

"I'm not a hussy, that's how."

"You know what I mean," Claire said playfully. She stared at him again, and Hailey wished she wouldn't, because she didn't want Jackson to think they were talking about him. "But what's he like? Does he have a girlfriend? I'm sure he has a girlfriend."

Claire's obsession with Jackson was starting to worry her. "You're a happily married woman, Claire. Aren't you?" She wasn't sure, given that her friend was so besotted by him.

"Yes, of course I am. I wouldn't dream of looking at anyone else, but Hales, he's so gorgeous," Claire whispered under her breath. "I'll never have eyes for anyone but Rudy, but I can look and admire. There's nothing wrong with that. So, *does* he?"

"Keep your voice down." Hailey put a finger to her lips. "Does he what?"

"Have a girlfriend," Claire cried.

"How would I know?" But she *did* know.

"You don't notice because you're surrounded by gorgeous hunks."

"They're not all that gorgeous once you get to know them. Most are, but you would be surprised."

"Tell me," Claire urged.

"I can't. I really can't. Sorry."

"I'm not going to tell anyone."

"It's a code," Hailey told her. Hollywood had its own code. You didn't snitch on people because their real lives would be such a shock compared to what they portrayed on the screen that the public wouldn't believe it. She wasn't one to stain another's reputation. "I can't reveal anyone's secrets. I wouldn't."

"But who's the best kisser and the nicest?"

Hailey winced. She had kissed her fair share of actors in

movies and had also been romantically linked with others. "I can't say."

"Rick Moretti?" Claire asked. "That Big Rick guy. He's all over the place."

She hadn't kissed him, not like that, not romantically. "He's sweet, and it's Big Rock."

"He is big and I'm sure he's all muscley and hard," Claire gushed. "Now *he* would be great in a bodyguard movie. I can see you and him together."

"No," she insisted. It was bad enough Val being on her back about Rick, she didn't need her friend to join in either.

CHAPTER 27

*A*s soon as the elevator doors closed, he pressed the button to ascend. The silence during the elevator ride was insufferable.

He wanted to ask her what happened when she had knocked the water over, because she had seemed extra jumpy. Uneasy almost.

She walked out first, then waited by the door as usual while he checked everything in her suite.

"Is this necessary?" she asked, her voice strained. He wondered what had made her mood even more sour. She and her friend had made a point to speak in hushed tones and he hadn't been able to hear a word.

"You know it's necessary." It was almost a growl, as if he were angry with her. She was with him, and yet there was no need for either of them to be angry. Or miserable, but that was how he felt.

Going from where they had been a few days ago to where they were now was like the difference in a child believing in Santa to being told that he had never existed in the first place.

"You won't have to do this for much longer," he told her. He was aware that her time here was almost at an end and that the movie premiere was in sight.

Roxy had been on his back about movie passes, and Patrick was still sore that he'd passed up a chance to introduce him to her. Jax had unwittingly promised him that he would ask Hailey about tickets to the movie premiere, but now he didn't feel he could even do that.

"Great. I can't wait to go back to my normal life."

"You can go back to living the high life."

"And you can go back to the mall."

He stared at her, surprised that she had hit so low but the telltale sign of her biting her lower lip told him she was lashing out.

She didn't mean it; that's what his gut told him, and he preferred to believe that.

The filming for the documentary had also finished and all that was left was the movie premiere which wasn't until the middle of next week.

Had things not changed, they would have spent the rest of their days together, but now everything had turned bleak. "You'll have to let me know what your plans are over the coming days."

"Sure." She closed the door on him.

She couldn't close the door fast enough. She pressed a hand to her chest, as if her heart had been bruised and needed healing. That she and Jackson had gone from an almost-kiss to this made her feel as if she had lost something precious that she could have taken better care of.

Her plans for the coming days? She had none. This had been the time she had been looking forward to, with Abe out of the picture, these would have been precious days when she and

Jackson could have spent time getting to know one another better.

There was nothing left to do now. She had to suffer through having him tailing her, and with the both of them being cold and distant, the fun had vanished from their relationship. Starling Bay had lost its allure. The excitement she had started to feel at the start of each day had fizzled out.

She was back to life in sleepy Starling Bay. She had lost her enthusiasm. Even the script which she had received this morning from Val for a 'serious' role had been left untouched.

She wasn't interested in that anymore.

Val had left a few messages on her phone, and there was also one from a number she didn't recognize. She replayed them now, sitting on her couch listlessly, wondering what to do with herself for the rest of the day.

The first message was from someone named Reed Knight. She opened her eyes because the name sounded familiar. He said something about the movie premiere and that he wanted to introduce himself. He looked forward to meeting her on the night.

Ugh.

That darned movie premiere. Next Wednesday evening.

She listened to Val's message, her voice went on like a babbling brook as she warbled on about Hailey's dress and the fabulous new jewelry that she was being loaned by a top designer from Rodeo Drive. Val said she would bring it with her on the morning of the premiere.

Jewelry. Was it even necessary here in Starling Bay? This wasn't a full-on Hollywood-style premiere. She didn't need all the usual razzmatazz.

Then Val mentioned something about the passes for the movie premiere. Hailey could have as many people attend as long as she submitted their names first. Her guests simply had to give their names at the door, and if they matched Hailey's list, they had access.

At least that was taken care of. She could let Jackson know that his sister and her friends could come.

But when could she let Jackson know? The idea caused her more grief than pleasure, given that they were in a standoff of sorts.

The idea of the premiere gave her grief. She didn't want it. She didn't really want to be here either.

Jax opened the door to find Patrick beaming at him. "Hey, dude, long time no see."

"What do you want?" Given his dour mood, it was the only thing he could think of to say.

"That's a great response. I come all this way to see how you are and this is what I get?"

His disappointment was less that he didn't like surprises, and more to do with the idea that he thought it might have been Hailey knocking on his door. "Come in," he said, his voice heavy with sarcasm as his friend cruised in and started on a mini tour of the hotel suite. "Wow! Roxy said it was amaze balls and it is."

"You've been speaking to my sister?"

Patrick picked up an apple from the fruit basket, polished it on his shirt sleeve and took a bite. "I got worried. I haven't seen you in a while. Ever since that mall signing event you tricked me out of."

Jax scratched his nose. "There was no underhanded trickery going on there, dude. I had to get Hailey out of there fast."

Patrick made himself at home on the couch, taking bites from the apple and looking around the room, an expression of approval on his face. "Whatever. This is the life. I can see that you've been having a great time while I've been busting my back at the mall."

"Busting your back?" Lifting wasn't part of their duties.

"The supervisor asked if I could help out with deliveries to some of the stores."

"That's not your job," Jax countered.

"He gave me overtime, and I needed the money." His friend took another apple bite. "Now this ..." his friend nodded as he surveyed the artwork on the walls, "this is the type of job I could really do with."

Jax hung his head. "Yeah, well. It's not all fun and games."

"You're just saying that to make me feel better."

His hands fell to his hips. There was no way he was going to convince his friend, and he didn't need to. It was enough that he'd come to know for himself, and now that he'd done this role, he would never do something like this again. The good times were a great high, but the down times were worse than the lowest lows.

"I'm not, but I don't expect you to believe me." He went to bed feeling miserable, woke up feeling the same, and today, waiting for Hailey to text her itinerary for the day had been like watching paint dry on a dull day. He knew she wasn't going to call and tell him anything; that ship had sailed to other waters.

He had considered quitting again many times this past week and the only thing that made him stay was knowing that he couldn't leave Hailey without the security that Val thought she needed. He still cared for the girl.

"Yeah, yeah, yeah. I still think you're lying." Patrick finished the apple, and looked thoroughly sated. "That was nice and sweet. Juicy too."

Jax rolled his eyes. "It is The Grand Hotel. What do you expect?"

Patrick's eyes twinkled. "What's it like living the high life? Being with her all day long?"

This was what Jax had been dreading. The details. "It's …" He swiped a hand to the back of his neck. "It's not all it's made out to be," he replied honestly.

"You're a liar."

"Believe what you want." But he could see why Patrick would think that. The truth was, aside from the fog that had now settled over them, being with Hailey had been a blast from his normal life and routine, and it had had nothing to do with going to any fancy places or doing anything extravagant. Watching TV and talking, having room service after a day in the woods or coming back from walks on the beach—all of these things were precious memories he would hold onto.

It wasn't something Patrick would understand.

Come to think of it, he wasn't sure why Patrick had come. It wasn't as if they could hang out. He couldn't go out or do anything. No going to the bar, no playing pool, no nothing.

"It's not the same without you," Patrick said. "When are you coming back?"

"This should be over soon. But I can't come back. I burned my bridges when I left in a rush."

"Are you serious?"

"I'm serious." He wasn't worried about finding a job. He'd find something. Or he'd get in touch with Reed Knight.

Patrick looked worried, more worried than Jax felt. The extra money from this job would tide him over for many months. "Don't worry. I'll find something."

"Something like this? This would look great for your resume. You could move to LA and be a bodyguard there." The grin on Patrick's face spread wide.

"Yeah, right. Somehow, I don't think so." As if this was something he could easily get up and do. As if he wanted to. "I don't want to move to LA, and I sure as hell don't want to do this for a living," he snapped.

"Yeah?" There were questions behind that one word.

Jax had given away more than he had intended to. He sniffed, trying to act as if he wasn't bothered. "Nah. It's not for me."

"I keep asking you. How was it?" Patrick kept asking.

"And I keep telling you, it was no big deal."

"No big deal?"

"If I could walk away from it now, I would."

Patrick stared at him in disbelief. "Do you mean that, or are you trying to play it down because of me?"

He meant it. He didn't want to mope around after Hailey and have the two of them be miserable and nasty to one another. It didn't help knowing that this time next week, she would probably have left Starling Bay. Where would that leave him if not with a few flimsy memories that didn't do him any good? Hailey would forget him as quickly as she snapped her fingers. That sucked, and he didn't like it. "It's not all it's cracked up to be. Anyway, look. I'm sorry I didn't get around to introducing you to her."

"It's not too late." Patrick shifted from the couch and strode confidently towards the door. "She's in, because you're in, so I'm going to introduce myself." He opened the door and was gone before Jax had a chance to say a word. As the realization hit him, he rushed out of his suite to find Patrick knocking on Hailey's door.

The knocking was loud and hard and urgent, and Hailey's heart somersaulted inside her chest.

It must be Jackson.

He wanted to clear the air.

Make up and start over.

A familiar wave of happiness slowly rolled up from the base of her stomach as she rushed to open the door. She jolted in shock, a lump of panic crawling up her throat as she stared at the face of a man she didn't recognize.

"Hey," Jackson's face suddenly appeared as he jostled the stranger out of the way.

"Hey! What did you go and do that for?" she heard the man say.

"Sorry about that. He wasn't supposed to do that. This is my friend, Patrick," said Jackson, while she fought to soothe her frayed nerves. "You might remember him from the bar that first night."

How could he be so laid back and at ease when she had been left wondering what had happened and why? Now it was too much to take in, the man, then Jackson, here now, at her door. She wasn't listening to his words but drinking in the sight of him; yearning for him. She had missed him, and now here he was.

Only, he hadn't come to see her.

"You scared her, you idiot," he hissed at his friend. His friend apologized, before smoothing down his hair and pulling his shirt down, straightening it. She remembered him. "You're the friend who I was supposed to meet at the mall that night?"

"That's the one. I'm Patrick. Nice to meet you." He held out his hand and she shook it. "Jax did a dirty on me. He said he would introduce us but then he whisked you away before I could say anything to you at the mall."

"He was under strict orders. Why don't you come in?" she suggested. The man looked slightly annoyed, and now that he was here, she might as well make amends.

"No ... no... it's okay ..." Jackson protested.

"Thank you, I will." Patrick elbowed Jackson out of the way and walked into her suite.

"Dude," Jackson hissed from the doorway, not taking a step further. He didn't look happy.

"He wants to come in. It's okay." She didn't understand his

reluctance to come in. It had been bad enough that he had been so distant lately, but the fact that he was continuing with this made her doubt all the thoughts and feelings she had had for him.

"This is some suite you've got here," Patrick said, walking around the room. "It's even better than his one." He jerked a thumb at Jackson. Hailey managed a smile. Jackson had stepped inside and had closed the door, but he seemed to be glued to the floor and didn't venture further inside.

"Hurry up and get your autograph," he said, when she and Patrick sat down and started talking.

"What's the rush?" Patrick asked him.

"Why don't you come and join us?" she suggested, deliberately putting him on the spot. "I've got nothing planned for today, and I'm sure that wall can prop itself up."

Patrick laughed at that, as if it were the funniest thing he'd heard all day.

"I have things to do." Jackson shot his friend a what-the-heck-are-you-doing glare.

"What things do you have to do?" Patrick clearly didn't want to move.

"Oh, before I forget." She jumped up and picked up the small notepad and pen which were lying on the coffee table. "If you give me your name, I'll make sure you can get into the movie theater for the premiere."

"You can do that?" Patrick asked, his eyes growing big as if he'd discovered he'd just won the lottery.

"I can do that."

He scribbled down his name quickly.

"It's easier this way for my publicist to coordinate. You can bring anyone you want." She glanced at Jackson. "Do you want to add Roxy's name? She can also bring anyone she wants."

Jackson looked peeved. "When were you going to tell me about this?"

"I meant to tell you earlier."

"When earlier?"

The floaty, jittery feeling in her stomach returned, only this time she wasn't sure if she was thrilled to be talking to him again, or annoyed that he was still sullen. This man dictated her moods and controlled her emotions, and he had no idea that he was doing so. "You haven't exactly been approachable, so I'm telling you now."

"It's good that Patrick turned up then, 'cause otherwise I might not have known." He shoved his hands in the pockets of his lounge pants. Dressed casually, he looked as handsome as ever.

That thing was back—the slow, simmering tension in the air between them. She could even feel the heat coming off his skin. She stepped back, scared that he would hear the hammering of her heart. "I would have eventually told you at some point. Things haven't been so great lately."

"I'm sensing some friction," Patrick noted. They both turned to him at the same time. "Definitely some friction." He walked over to the fruit basket and picked up a pear. "You don't mind if I help myself, do you?"

"Go ahead," Hailey replied.

"Too late for that now," she heard Jackson grumble. "This guy is driving me nuts. Dude," he hissed. "We should go."

She could see that he was in an irritable mood, that he didn't want to be in her room if he could help it. "It's fine. He's been waiting to meet me. Just let him chill a while."

"He's only met you for ten minutes and now he's making himself at home."

"You sound jealous," she said, testing him.

"Of what?" he said, keeping his tone low while Patrick admired the flowers in all the vases. She thought it best not to answer that.

Patrick bit into his pear and made an approving noise "Where do they get their fruit from? It's delicious."

Jackson opened the door, getting ready to leave.

"He's in a hurry. I have no idea why he's in a hurry," Patrick said to her. "Have I missed something? Is something going –"

"Dude!" Jackson's voice made her jump, but it appeared not to have any effect on his friend.

"He was ready to quit this job," Patrick told her, calmly biting into the pear as he walked past her.

Her mouth fell open in shock. "You were going to quit?" she asked Jackson. Had she really gotten it all so wrong?

Jackson coughed in answer and this told her everything. He really had considered leaving. She felt numb, her legs suddenly going weak. What had made him hate her so much that he couldn't stand to be near her?

"Yeah," Patrick replied, taking another bite. "He really was. He asked me if I wanted to step in. Not that it would have happened," he said smoothly, no doubt seeing the look of shocked horror on her face. "Imagine, me being your bodyguard instead of him. But I don't have a black belt in martial arts, and I sure don't have those muscles. You're still safe while Jax is around, don't you worry."

Jackson's jawline tensed. "We. Should. Leave. *NOW*." He looked as if he was going to box this man's ears as soon as he got away from there.

"You really said that?" she asked again.

"You're leaving soon, anyway," Jackson replied. "I'm going to have to find other work."

"But you were thinking of leaving now, before your time was up?" Another long spell of silence followed. She wondered if he was thinking back to that last evening when Roxy had shown up. Everything had turned miserably wrong after that.

She stared up at him and tried not to let her gaze settle on the green of his eyes, or on his slightly longish hair which he'd swept back. It showed off more of his angular features.

She had never seen Jackson look so angry. "If you don't move right now, I will throw you over my shoulder and—"

Patrick moved fast. "It was good to meet you, Hailey. See you at the premiere."

CHAPTER 29

"What the heck do you think you're doing?" Jax slammed the door shut once Patrick was safely ensconced inside his suite.

Patrick looked confused. "What did I do?"

Jax took one look at the almost-eaten pear, and then glanced at Patrick's smug face. He had a good mind to throw him out. "Who told you to go and announce that I wanted to leave?"

"I knew something was up when I got here. You've been so uptight and moody."

"That's because I haven't had a day off in weeks." He missed going for a drink, meeting his friends, shooting pool. This job was okay when things were fine, but at times like now, with him and Hailey at odds, the atmosphere was too intense. He didn't like it.

"You're grumpy and moody and mean."

Jax turned his head so fast towards his friend that he almost gave himself whiplash. "What are you talking about?"

Patrick ignored the question. "I see it now."

"See what?" he asked gruffly.

"Why Roxy asked me to check in on you."

Jax let out a huge sigh. Roxy and her big mouth.

Patrick licked his fingers. "She said she wasn't sure, but she thought you had the hots for Hailey Ross. I can confirm it, now that I've seen it with my own eyes. I think she likes you too, the way she was looking up at you with those sad big blue eyes of hers."

"She does not."

"You're too dumb to see it."

"I'm not too dumb to know that she and I aren't going to work."

"That's the difference between you and me, Jax. I can look at a poster of Hailey Ross and fall in love with her, but someone like you would think I'm an idiot. You'd think I don't have a chance with a gal like that. I reckon you think the same about yourself, even though you have no reason to, looking the way you do with your pecs and biceps and all."

"You're talking a load of bull, Patrick. She's taken your name for the guest list, you're going to the movie premiere, so you can leave now."

"Stubborn too, as well as dumb," Patrick huffed on his way out.

It got Jax thinking. He was proud and stubborn, but also afraid of looking like a fool, and of being vulnerable. Dumb? No.

Hailey had looked worried when she'd opened the door and seen Patrick. But that worry had vanished as soon as Jax had appeared and her eyes had lit up, as if she was happy to see him.

He had laughed at Patrick for staring at Hailey Ross in those posters at the mall and thinking that he had a chance with her.

Turns out fate had favored him instead, but he was letting all the things people told him get in the way. He was throwing away a chance to be happy, even for the next few days. He didn't have to think about long-term because who knew what lay ahead? But there was no point in being afraid to grab a chance of happiness now.

He decided it was now or never and marched towards the door before he convinced himself to change his mind. As he opened the door, Hailey was standing on the other side, ready to knock.

She looked surprised, then confused. "I hadn't even knocked yet."

"What's the matter?" he asked, as always worried about her safety and whether something had happened.

"Why did you open the door?"

He could lie. He could deflect the real reason, after all, she had come to him, but time was short, and he was sick of playing games. "I was coming to apologize."

"For?"

He scratched his neck. "For the way I've been. I didn't mean to take it out on you. I was going to say sorry." He watched her face, needing to see how she would react. Needing to know if Patrick had been right; that she did feel something for him. He had believed she did, because of those almost-kisses, but sometimes the mind played tricks. He needed to be sure.

"I was coming to say the same." She folded her arms.

"I don't want our last few days to be like this," he said.

"Me neither."

"How about another truce?"

She nodded. "I'm sorry about Val, and that you heard what she said. She doesn't know you, not like I do, and you shouldn't take any notice of her."

"My sister said I should stay away from you."

"I could tell she didn't like me."

"She's only looking out for me—"

"Looking out for you?" Hailey cried. "What does she think I'm going to do with you?"

He had been stupid to listen to her. "Rox isn't a bad person, she just doesn't want me to get hurt." He motioned for her to come in so that they could discuss this properly, in private. "The last time you came over, when Roxy was here, I wasn't prepared."

"Prepared for what?" she asked.

"Prepared for you to show up like that, or for my nosy sister to be here and have something to say about you."

"What did she have to say?"

"Roxy always has something to say." It was unfortunate but true. She had a good heart, but she also had a way about her that some found abrasive. "It's not important now."

"When I walked in that day, it felt as if the two of you had some inside joke on me."

"An inside joke on you?" he asked, incredulous. He lifted a hand to her face. "You think I would make a joke about you?"

"Didn't you?"

"I was caught in an uncomfortable situation. You and me … at the lake, and then in your room …" They'd almost kissed for the second time. If he had been a superstitious man, he would have taken this to mean something. But Val and Roxy had done as good a job to convince him that he and Hailey had no part in being together. "I'm sorry I was so cold to you then."

"I came over to apologize for what Val said. I know you heard her."

"The truth hurts."

"What truth? Val doesn't speak the truth, it's just her opinion," Hailey countered.

"She was reminding you of who you are, and who I am."

"And what's that?"

The last time he'd called her a Hollywood star, she had hated the label, but that was the truth of their situation. She was a Hollywood star. Just like he was a security guard. "We're so different, Hailey. I don't know if this can work."

"You have such little faith."

"I've been hurt before," he confessed.

"So have I. Don't push me away, Jackson. I've met men you and Val would think were perfect for me—"

He ground down on his teeth. The idea of her with someone else made his insides turn to ice. "Yeah, and who might that be? Someone like Big Rock?" His tone had turned hard again. "I hate the idea of you and someone else."

"There is no me and someone else. There's just you ... if we don't get interrupted again ..." She inched closer to him and he couldn't resist lifting his hand to her face. Her skin was soft and warm, her eyes shining. With her lips slightly parted, the temptation to try to kiss her again was stronger than ever.

She hadn't told him to move his hand away, nor had she asked him what the heck he was doing. She was staring up at him as if that was exactly what he should be doing.

Licking his lower lip instinctively, he lowered his head a little, so-so-slowly, mindful of every little heartbeat, every breath as he rubbed his thumb across her cheek. She tilted her head, a confirmation that she liked his touch.

Then he kissed her. He pressed his mouth gently against hers and fell into the softness of her touch, the allure of her scent, the warmth of her skin. It felt like falling into heaven. A few seconds later, when he opened his eyes and he pulled away, it took a while before her eyelids fluttered open.

He had finally done it. He had kissed Hailey Ross, and it had been magical. "I missed you," she said, sliding her arms possessively around his waist.

"I've missed you. I've missed talking to you," he murmured. "I can't tell with you, Hailey. I'm not sure what you want. What you feel."

"I feel *you*."

He stared down at her upturned face. "My sister told me I had no business being interested in you."

"You told her you were?"

"Roxy knew. Call it women's intuition."

"Or a big sister's knowing."

"Would yours know?" he asked her.

"You know I have a sister?" She seemed surprised.

"I know mostly everything about you," he confessed. He pulled her further towards him and tightened his arms around her waist. It wasn't long before they fell into another sweet and seductive kiss again.

"I've been so miserable these past few days. I hate not being with you, Jackson," she said, when they broke apart for air.

"You really mean that?" The blood rushed through his veins, adrenaline pumping through him. He felt as if he'd been given the kiss of life.

"I hate not being with you."

His smile widened. He tightened his hold around her, she leaned in closer so that they were touching. "I've been a miserable, moody, whiny monster," he told her.

This was too much talking, of the getting-to-know-you type, the kind of talking they could do when they were sitting on the couch or having dinner. Not the type of conversation to be had right now. Not in this perfect moment. He lowered his head, eyeing her perfectly luscious lips. An unwelcome thought flashed through his mind: Hollywood actors had kissed those lips.

But that had all been a pretense.

This was real.

Her smile brightened. This time, he couldn't resist, with her upturned face and her lips so full and inviting, he looked into her eyes and kissed her.

The kiss deepened, and every delicious feeling of attraction that they had been hiding from one another tumbled forth. She left him breathless. "I'm crazy about you," he whispered before he kissed her again.

CHAPTER 30

She had kissed many of Hollywood's sexiest men, but she had never, *ever* been kissed like that before. It had been worth the wait.

He turned up at her door the next morning. "Do you have anything on the agenda today?"

"Nothing. I haven't made any plans. I wasn't in the mood for doing much. I haven't been in the mood to do anything, ever since …" She didn't need to spell it out because she knew he understood, because he'd told her he felt the same. "We have a few days."

"A few days? Then we should make the most of them. We could go to your favorite place. You might not get a chance to go again."

"Now? As in right now?" She stared at him in disbelief.

"You don't do spontaneous. Here's your chance. We can hop on my bike and be there in twenty. Do you want to go?"

"To the lake?" Yes. She did.

They were there less than half an hour later and they walked and talked for hours in the woods, catching up again. She told him about the messages that Val had left her, and that she had also heard from someone named Reed Knight.

"The movie premiere," he mumbled, his voice sounding a little sad. She knew why. The movie premiere signaled the end of her visit here. It meant that she would soon be leaving.

Odd to think that she was the movie actress, and he was the bodyguard because their roles seemed to have suddenly changed. Now she was in deference to him.

"When is Val coming?" he asked.

"On the day of the premiere."

"That's good news." He smiled at her. It was good news. It meant they had more time to spend together to make up for these last few days they had lost. She was starting to look forward to the premiere, because with Jackson by her side, it would take on another meaning.

"Val will bring a team of makeup artists and hairdressers who will completely transform me," she complained. There would be hours of preparation and she would be preened and primped until she emerged looking strikingly beautiful.

"You don't need to be transformed. You're stunning the way you are."

She squeezed his hand. "But the dress will be glamorous, and I'll have to do it justice."

"You will. It's always about the dress, isn't it?" He looked happy again, and with a light in his eyes. Everything was back to normal again and the simmering resentment she had sensed from him had disappeared. "Unfortunately, in Hollywood, the dresses for these events are a big deal."

"Unfortunately? Why do you say that? I thought you women liked your dresses and your fancy trinkets."

"We do, but these things don't seem like such a big deal anymore." There was a time when she used to get excited about the dress, and the jewels—borrowed from Hollywood's exclusive jewelers on loan, and then she would have a bodyguard or two guarding her like a second skin for the evening, be it at the Oscars or the Emmys, or some other red-carpet affair. But she didn't care about the dress or anything else. The things which would keep Val awake at night had no significance for her.

It warmed her soul that she and Jackson had made up and were moving on to better things. With an end in sight to her visit here, a sadness tinged her newfound happiness, but she didn't want to think about that now.

He lifted his wrist, checked his watch. "We should get back, it's getting late."

"Can we have a look at the gift shop?" She wanted to buy a few things for her friends back home.

They walked into the shop and looked around. There were pretty ornaments and some Easter-themed baskets filled with cute chicks and brightly colored eggs. There were lots of other things too, plates and cups with pictures of Starling Bay.

"So many pretty things," she murmured, picking up an ornament. A shop assistant came over and asked if she needed any help. Hailey told her she was just looking. She had picked up a cup and was examining that when the assistant told her that Dylan, the shop owner, made them in his workshop in the back.

"He *made* them?" Hailey lifted up a cup. It was bright yellow with a chick's face on it.

"He's a potter," she explained. "He made those vases as well." The assistant pointed to a display table in the corner.

"Clever dude." Jackson came over and examined a bowl.

"That's pretty," she commented. It was bright yellow, and it matched the cup she was holding. She picked another one up so that she had two. He picked up another breakfast bowl as well. "For when you come over for breakfast."

When and where this breakfast would take place she had no

idea, but it pleased her that he had said it. "Do you have any jewelry?" he asked the lady. "I'm looking for something pretty."

"It's funny you should ask because ..." and the two of them disappeared out of Hailey's sight. She continued to look around. There were so many gift ideas that she soon had her shopping basket full.

"Like it?" Jackson asked her, reappearing some time later. He held up a delicate choker in front of her eyes. It was purple and green, and looked like it was made of glass.

"I love it!" she cried. It was so gorgeous.

"Good, because I bought it for you. And look ..." He held it closer to her. In the middle, suspended from a loop, were the letters J and H, their initials, in gold.

"Oh, Jackson." She didn't know what to say. To her, this was more precious than anything from Tiffany. "I *love* it. That's so thoughtful of you."

"He was lucky," said the shop owner, suddenly appearing out of nowhere. She recognized him from the other day. "That was the last of the chokers. We have plenty of letters, though."

"It's beautiful." She was picky with jewelry and had a certain eye for things. She didn't want something too bold and loud and flashy and preferred understated and unique pieces, like the choker Jackson had presented her with. She was genuinely touched by his thoughtfulness, and the fact that he had managed to find something in a gift shop like this of all places.

"I didn't realize this was your store," she said.

"I've had it a few years. Now I run it with my wife, Merry."

Hailey looked around. "Is she around?!" She liked this friendly couple and wanted to say 'hi'.

"She's taking a break." Dylan started to ring up the gifts she had bought and, one by one, started packing them with tissue paper so that the delicate items wouldn't break.

"And that big—"

"Spartacus?" He put the items into two bags. "He's lying at her feet, probably." He rang up the price and she paid. "You have a lovely gift shop. Your assistant said you make a lot of these items."

"I do. I'm better with my hands than I was anything else."

"You're very talented."

"Thank you. I'll say the same to you."

Jackson took the bags from her. "Dylan knows Reed, the guy I do some side jobs for sometimes. The guy who you said left you a message on your phone."

Hailey recalled the name and remembered the two of them mentioning this the last time they met. "What a small world." It truly was. People were so connected to one another here. Everyone knew everyone else.

"We're looking forward to the premiere," Dylan said.

"You're coming?" To her surprise, it seemed that everyone she met was going to be there.

"We are coming. My stepdaughter, Chloe, loves your movies."

Hailey beamed at him. "That's so sweet. I look forward to seeing you all there."

"We're looking forward to it."

Jackson stared at the bags he was carrying.

"What's wrong?" she asked as they turned to leave.

"We're not going to be able to get all that home on my bike."

"I'll call you a cab. It will be here in about five minutes," Dylan said.

Problem solved.

"Thank you."

They left the shop and walked over to the bike where she took the bags off Jackson.

"I'll wait with you," he told her, before reaching into the pocket of his shirt. "Put your bags down."

"What? Why?"

He had pulled out the choker. "Do you really like it?"

"I love it."

"You're not just saying that? Because I can change it, if you want. It's not gold or diamonds or—"

"I. Love. It." She really did, though she could tell that he still seemed uncertain. It would take time for him to see that money and material things didn't matter to her as much as he seemed to think they did—and while this was easy to say now that she had no financial worries—she was also more worldly wise to know that money didn't bring happiness. "If I didn't like it, I would have told you."

"Promise?"

"Yes. I will never lie to you, Jackson, I promise. *We* should never lie to one another."

"Straight up honesty," he said, bending down and landing a sweet kiss on her lips. "Turn around," he instructed. She did, and he slipped the choker around her neck. She felt his fingers brush her nape as he fastened it. She turned around, her fingers feeling the 'J' and 'H'. "I love it, Jackson. Thank you."

He kissed her. "It looks good on you, and you're welcome."

CHAPTER 31

Things had turned around so quickly, he felt as if his head was spinning. It was all due to this gorgeous creature curled up on the couch with him.

Fed up with room service, they ordered takeout from Fellini's when they got back. This was the place Hailey had gone to the other day with her friend, when she had spilled the water all over the table. Jax didn't care much about fancy places or fancy food —or so he thought, but it turned out that there was something to be said for fancy food. It was freaking amazing.

Now that they were back together again, he had an inkling of the good times ahead, with a woman he had believed he didn't deserve. It had taken his good friend, Patrick, the man he'd practically thrown out of his suite, to show him that he was entitled to be with Hailey.

They talked long into the night, kissed long into the night, and when it was time for him to leave, around 4:00 a.m. in the morning, Hailey begged him to stay.

"I can't stay. You know that." The kissing hadn't stopped, but he wasn't about to push the boundaries and move fast so soon.

"You said you were protecting me." She sat up on the couch

on her knees, putting her arms around his neck and reeling him in for another kiss. "If you sleep on the couch, I'll feel so much safer." When she kissed him again, he had been unable to refuse.

So, he stayed over and slept on the couch.

They spent the next few days like this, in a fairy tale bubble, just the two of them, talking and watching TV, ordering takeout, going for walks along the beach and around the town. Catching up. He only returned to his room to take a shower and get a fresh change of clothes.

He could get used to this, not *this*, staying in a place like The Grand Hotel, but being with Hailey. He forgot that she was this successful movie star, because to him she was *just* Hailey, and just Hailey was all he wanted.

This had to have been the best part of her stay here.

The other parts, the less fun ones such as Abe and his questions, seemed so far away that they might as well have been another lifetime ago.

Time had slowed down, not in a frozen, paralytic way, but slow enough that their days were lazy and simple, and though they only had a few, they seemed to stretch out longer. She would lie on the couch with Jackson, either snuggled up in his arms, or on her side as they watched TV.

They talked about their pasts, their failed relationships, their broken hearts, and then they kissed and made plans etched in hopes and dreams. Plans for how things could be.

She was aware that living in this cozy little cocoon would make it that much harder for her to emerge from it and get back to reality.

One evening they were lying on their sides on the couch, a bowl of popcorn on the coffee table, the TV on. She stretched out, raising one arm into the air. Behind her, Jackson slid his hand along her waist and tickled her. She erupted in a fit of giggles.

It was domestic bliss. She could imagine this being her life for real with Jackson. Logistics had to be worked out, but it wasn't impossible to think of a future that looked something like this.

He pulled her back against him. "You fit against me like we're two pieces of a puzzle."

"Awww." She turned on her back, lifted her hand to sweep back a lock of his hair that had fallen forward. "You say the most romantic things."

"That's because you bring out the Mr. Romantic in me."

They kissed again, then stopped at the sound of a knock on the door.

"Someone knocked," she whispered.

"I heard it."

"Room service?"

"We haven't ordered anything yet," he reminded her. He strode towards the door in his bare feet, tidying his hair, and straightening down his vest. She sat up, her arms around her knees, bracing herself.

He opened the door, and then Val appeared. She didn't appear as much as she swept into the room. "Well, hello—" Val stopped, her mouth open as she surveyed the scene. In one hand she carried an outfit, which Hailey presumed was her dress in a garment bag. "What's this?" Val spun around, looked at Jackson, her pointed gaze taking in the length of him before she turned back around and did the same to Hailey. "What's going on?" her voice was deathly quiet. Hailey stood up slowly, disbelief souring her mood. Their entire evening was ruined and the rest of her short time with Jackson was over.

"What are you doing here?" she asked. "You told me you were coming on Wednesday morning."

"The movie premiere is on Wednesday."

"I know. But you said you were coming in the morning," Hailey reminded her. Instead, Val had arrived two days early. It was too much. She didn't want to spend her time with Val when she had plans to do nothing and be with Jackson. "Why didn't you call me?" At least then she would have been prepared.

"It's a good thing I didn't." Val glared at Jackson "Care to explain what's going on?"

Hailey didn't want Jackson to get the blame for anything. "We're just hanging out, watching TV."

"Watching TV?" Val didn't seem convinced. "This is not what I meant when I said you needed to guard her with your life," she snapped at Jackson.

"What part are you having problems with, exactly?" Jackson shot back.

"Is something going on, Hailey?" Val asked, but Hailey was too flustered to reply. She hadn't had time to think, she had never expected this. "This has nothing to do with you, Val. This is my personal life."

"The studio owns you, Hailey. You have a blockbuster movie which hasn't done as well as it was supposed to and—"

"That's because of the helicopter crash and the delay. You can't pin that on me." She didn't understand this angle, why Val would say that.

"I'm going," Jackson said to her. He looked as disappointed as she felt.

"Don't," she pleaded, then to Val, "Where are you staying?"

"On the next floor down. Jax, your services are no longer required."

Hailey couldn't believe her ears. "You can't fire him!" In a few moments, everything that had been wonderful had suddenly crashed and died. "He hasn't done anything wrong."

"We have work to do, and you have the premiere to prepare for."

"I've got plenty of time for that, and it's days away yet."

"The studio manages your commitments and appearances, Hailey. Please don't be difficult. I need your cooperation."

Val's words fell on her like debris from a plane wreck. "Difficult? I don't see how I'm being difficult. And what do you mean by cooperation?"

"I'll talk to you in private." Val turned to Jackson. "Jax, please take your belongings and vacate the room right now."

"What? No! You can't do that." Hailey's gut hardened to stone.

"I plan to move in early tomorrow once they've given it a good clean." Val didn't seem to hear or care. Hailey wasn't sure which it was.

"What about Hailey's protection?" Jackson asked.

"She doesn't require the type of protection you've been giving her."

Inflamed by the way Val spoke of her, as if she wasn't here, Hailey marched to Jackson's side. "He's not going anywhere."

"I've fired him."

"You can't. I *need* him."

Val shook her head. "We have things to do."

Hailey reached for Jackson's hand, and clasped it tightly. "He's living here with me, and he'll stay here."

"He's *what?*"

Jackson let go of her hand. "It's not what you think. I slept on the couch."

"You slept here?" Val shrieked.

Jackson moved towards the door and Hailey rushed to him. "Don't go. You don't have to go." She turned her back on Val, who had draped the dress over the couch and taken a seat.

"I should go," he whispered. "Now isn't a good time. You and her need to figure things out."

"You and me need to figure things out," she insisted. She

would not tolerate this, Jackson leaving just because Val had decided to come early and was babbling nonsense about cooperation. She didn't care.

Jackson lowered his head as if he was about to kiss her, then stopped. "Call me when you can talk."

She put her finger to his lips. "I will."

"What's gotten into you, Hailey?" Val demanded. Hailey lowered her head, not wanting or needing this disturbance to her life. She folded her arms and eyed Val. "You are my publicist and my agent, but you are not indispensable."

"Your career could do with a little lift." Val got up and walked towards Hailey. "I want to see you stay where you belong, at the top, Hailey. Not throwing it all away by having some fun times with a loser."

"He's not a loser. Don't you dare call him that."

"You're bored. I get it. There's nothing here for you, and nothing to do. You're just having fun, but remember there's no future in this."

Hailey frowned. There had been a sudden turn in the events. She had missed something, been out of the loop for too long all the way here in Starling Bay. "What are you talking about?"

"You're tired." Val walked towards the door and Hailey felt a touch of relief that this woman would soon be gone. "We'll talk tomorrow."

"I'm not tired," she snapped. "I'm annoyed. I'm mad, I'm enraged that you're here, and frankly, I'm disgusted by the way you've treated Jackson."

"I'm here to help you."

She folded her arms, trying to keep calm. "I'm not sure I want your help."

"You're angry because I messed up your evening, Hailey, but I came early so that we could go over your second round of publicity."

"What second round of publicity?"

"As I keep telling you, the movie isn't doing as well as had been projected."

"Is that all my fault?" The movie had been delayed due to reasons out of anyone's control. Maybe this was a sign for her to not give up and to continue going after those serious roles she coveted. "I don't even want to do those types of roles anymore."

"Those roles buy you your multi-million-dollar homes in all the best places. They're the reason you drive the cars you do and wear the clothes you have."

"Maybe I don't need more money. Maybe there's more to life than that."

Val headed towards the door. "Like I said, you're tired. We'll talk in the morning. I'm downstairs if you need me." Hailey closed the door, her façade of stoic resilience falling as her anger resurfaced. In the next moment she rushed out and knocked on Jackson's door, but he didn't answer.

Her stomach churned. He couldn't have moved out that fast, could he? She knocked harder, her desperation making her anxious. "Jackson!" But he never came to the door. She should have known that he wouldn't have hung around, not after what Val had said, and knowing the type of man he was she could hardly blame him.

The tension along his jawline moved down to his shoulders and hardened along his back. He was a walking wall of brick. That damn woman had not only ruined their evening, she had been rude and disrespectful. He needed to go out in order to calm himself down.

He rode all the way to Clearwater Forest and back again, trying to make sense of all that had happened. He had known from before, from the last time he had overheard Val on the phone, that she wasn't keen on him and Hailey developing a friendship. Except now it wasn't just a friendship. It went deeper, had moved beyond to something that could become stronger. But meeting Val had been unsettling. The woman clearly didn't like him.

As a bodyguard, yes.

As Hailey's boyfriend, no.

And she'd gone and fired him too.

He wasn't worried about that as much as he was worried about Hailey. He was also concerned about her protection, and for her having to face that witch. Tempers had flared high, and the air had been thick with tension, he'd decided it would be best for him to leave.

So much for him and Hailey spending what little time they had together. But he could wait it out. The premiere would be over soon, and he'd let Hailey contact him when the coast was clear.

She was worth the wait.

The next day, eager to speak to Roxy, he went to the diner early in the morning before any of her employees turned up.

"What are you doing here?" his sister asked. She had a coffee pot in her hand and was getting ready to pour.

"You should pour that cup," he cautioned, pulling out a chair at one of the tables nearby.

"Why?" She looked at him carefully. "You look like hell, Jax. Sit down and tell me what's going on." She got another cup out and poured coffee for them both.

"I've been fired."

"What?" Roxy's face twisted in anger. "That nasty little airhead!"

"Don't. Call. Her. That."

"What did she go and fire you for?"

"She didn't fire me. Her manager, agent, or whatever, she showed up."

"And she fired you?" Roxy's eyebrows squashed together. "What the hell for?" He had hoped to keep secret his and Hailey's new romance. It was nobody's business, and it was still so new and fragile that he needed to protect it. If he wasn't careful, his sister would wrangle it out of him somehow. "Because we were watching TV together."

Roxy tilted her head, and he could see the cogs in her brain turning. She narrowed her eyes. "Watching TV?"

"Yeah." He sipped his coffee. "It was just TV."

"You're don't get fired for watching TV, even if that's not something that bodyguards do."

He stared back at Roxy, tried to keep his gaze casual, which wasn't easy given that he hadn't slept much. Val's words kept replaying in his head, making him want to lash out at something. Roxy would see right through him. She always did.

"I like her." There. He'd gone and said it. "I like her and I can't help it."

"I. Knew. It." Disapproval was set in the press of Roxy's lips, but there was something else, too. Concern. Not concern about him losing the job. Concern that he might get hurt. She had always looked out for her little bro, as she called him, even though she was so much smaller, compared to him. "You didn't take my advice, did you?"

"I tried to keep it in mind." He'd had his guard up, but Hailey Ross had managed—through no fault of her own, through no scheming way of trying to get his attention—to penetrate it.

"You didn't try hard enough."

"I didn't come here for you to lecture me, Rox. I don't care about the job."

"You don't care about the job?" She folded her arms. "It's only ever about the job, Jax. Think about it. How are you going to pay the rent?"

She was so focussed on survival, she couldn't see anything else. He'd been so livid, so confused, he'd needed to speak to someone which was why he'd come here, but maybe it had been a mistake. "The job was going to finish soon anyway. I like her, Rox. I really like her. I know what you said about her, but Hailey's not like that. She's not a diva. She doesn't show off. She hates me calling her a superstar. She's not 'the' Hailey Ross. She's just Hailey, and if you got to know her, if you stopped hating on her, you might find that she's a nice person too."

Roxy's eyes softened, her face losing its mask of skepticism. "You really like her?"

"I'm crazy about her."

"So quickly?"

"I'm with her most of the day. It doesn't seem so quick to me."

"But you barely know her. What you see is a front."

"And she let it down."

"She's—"

"Famous, and a movie star, I know."

"And she'll go back to—"

"I know."

"This has no future—"

"I don't know that. *You* don't know that."

They locked defiant gazes, ping-ponging their verbal assessments back and forth.

"What does Hailey say?" Roxy asked him, finally.

"We haven't talked about it." It was new, this restart. Their journey had been stop-start the entire way.

"You really like her?"

He nodded.

Roxy pinched the bridge of her nose. "Oh, Jax. What have you gotten yourself into?"

"I don't know. I'm crazy about this girl, and I had to tell someone."

She smiled. "You don't usually run your girlfriends by me."

"She's different, and she's important enough that I want to."

"I just don't want you to get hurt, Jax. That's all."

"If you gave her a chance, if you made an effort to get to know her, you would like her too."

"I don't hate her, Jax. I don't know her."

"You haven't exactly been warm and friendly towards her, even though you were greedy enough to ask her for tickets to the premiere."

Roxy threw her hands in the air in defeat. "So sue me." She shrugged. "It just seems as if some girls have all the luck. Hailey was one of the pretty ones at school. You know the type that gets all the attention. And then she goes and gets this dream career, and she has everything. *Everything.*"

Knowing what he did about Hailey, and her insecurities, and the pressure to look good always, and the pressure for every movie to be a success, this was most definitely not true. "It's not as easy as you think."

Roxy rolled her eyes. "She doesn't have to get up at 6:00 a.m. every morning and get ready for work."

"She has to get up at 4:00 a.m. on days when she's filming."

"You're going to defend her no matter what I say."

"I'm trying to make you see that it's not always as glamorous as you think."

"I don't want to fight, Jax. If you like her, I'm sure she's nice. I'm sorry I haven't been friendly to her. It's hard to be happy when, no matter how hard I work, I don't seem to get a break."

He recognized defeat and worry in Roxy's tired eyes. "What's going on?"

"Things aren't so great here."

"What? Why didn't you tell me?" He sat forward, hearing this for the first time.

"Because I'm going to make this work no matter what. I just never thought it would be such hard work taking over from mom and dad."

"But I thought you were doing well?"

"I'm doing okay. Getting by, but I can't seem to do better. I've been stagnating. Nothing I do seems to be working."

He felt guilty, not only for not asking, but for not being here for her. He'd been so wrapped up in his own drama. "Want me to come and work here? I'm free now." He grinned.

"No. Don't be silly."

"I'll work for free."

"Naturally." The corners of her mouth curved up into a smile. "I have no intention of paying you, like always."

"Some things never change."

"But you can eat all you want."

"I know." Now that he looked more closely, he could see the dark circles under her eyes. "We'll figure something out, Rox. Don't worry. Roxy's Diner will be fine."

"I know it will. I have every intention of making this place amazing."

"Hailey's put your name down on the guest list for the premiere," he told her.

"Then I'd better get myself something nice to wear. What about you? You're coming, aren't you?"

He lifted his coffee cup. Val might have fired him, but she wasn't going to stop him from going to the premiere.

CHAPTER 33

*I*t was a circus and the phone hadn't stopped ringing, along with Val's cell phone.

Hailey's entire suite had now been overtaken by others. Val was in the corner making calls, and the makeup artist and hairdresser were busy working their magic on her. The makeup artist's assistant was fretting over the dress and it getting creased.

This was what people worried about?

She was thankful that it was the day of the premiere. She had managed to survive a day alone with Val yesterday. A lot of it was griping, with her and Val butting heads over the types of roles she wanted, which Val still tried to talk her out of. She reminded herself that it could have been a lot worse. Val could have come a week early, especially since she loved Starling Bay. Worse, she and Jackson might not have made up by the time Val arrived, thwarting their attempts to get back together forever.

Things had happened for a reason, and as they were meant to. She just had to find a meaning in all this and move through it.

When she got the chance, she'd managed to call Jackson and they had spoken for hours on the phone. It would have to do for now. What helped her to deal with things better was knowing that this would all be over tonight.

Val was heading back to LA first thing tomorrow morning. They'd had another strained conversation when Hailey had announced that she was going to stay on for a few more weeks. She wanted to pick up from where she and Jackson had been so rudely halted.

Val had said there was something she had wanted to discuss with her, but they had been interrupted with phone call after phone call.

Hailey sat in her chair and tried to breathe through the chaos and pandemonium. Closing her eyes allowed her to imagine Jackson, and the way he made her feel. Seeing him at the premiere later would be enough to calm her nerves.

It was only a matter of hours. There was the meet and greet at the movie theater at the start, where she would finally get to meet Reed Knight. Val had told her that some movie people were flying in from LA just to watch the movie, but they were heading home once it finished. Camera crews had also been setting up outside the theater. This had surprised her because all along Val had said the Starling Bay premiere would be a small affair.

With so much noise going on, she didn't even hear the knock at the door until Val rose sharply and announced that she would get it.

Hailey looked in the mirror, unable to turn around while the hairdresser styled her hair. Her heart skipped a beat as Val opened the door, which she could see from the reflection of the huge mirror that the makeup artist had put up. She raised her hand for the hairdresser to stop.

"I was beginning to think you must have gotten lost," she heard Val say. A man walked in, tall and muscular. Hailey swiveled around on her chair to get a better look, but to her disappointment it wasn't Jackson.

Val ushered him in and sat him down, then clapped her hands excitedly, ordering the man to hurry up. He opened his briefcase and pulled something out.

Hailey knew, as soon as she saw the familiar black velvet box. This was why the Man in Black had shown up; her new bodyguard. He would guard the million-dollar jewels that had been loaned to her.

"Look!" Val rushed over to her and with the box open, and proudly displayed the sparkling diamond jewelry inside. "Your necklace, earrings, and bracelet." Her eyes were all lit up and she peered into the box as if she wanted to devour it. "This is Dimitri. He's here to—"

Hailey turned her nose up at the jewely. "I know what he's here for, but I'm not wearing *that*."

"What? What do you mean, you're not wearing that?"

She fingered the familiar J and H. "I've got my necklace." She hadn't taken it off ever since Jackson had given it to her.

Val's face crumpled in disgust. "You're not wearing that cheap little choker."

"I am." Hailey's voice was calm and confident. Val had ruined her last few days, and now she was going to take pleasure in ruining hers. "I'll wear the earrings and bracelet, but I'm not wearing the necklace. I told you. I already have one."

Val glared at her.

"Is this what you wanted to talk to me about?" Hailey asked.

Val lifted her chin, her lips twisting. "You're being difficult again."

Hailey held the gaze. "You've made all of this difficult for me from the moment you arrived."

She sat back and nodded at the hairdresser to resume styling her hair.

~

"Look at you!" Roxy's eyes widened so much Jax was scared they'd fly right out of their sockets.

She had come over to his place and had agreed to drive them to the movie theater. Patrick was due to arrive at any moment.

"You like it?" he asked, pointing at his tux. He had to admit, he did look good.

"If you want to make an impression on your new girlfriend, that is definitely the way to go."

Roxy wasn't one to shower people with compliments, and the fact that she had only confirmed to him that he looked good.

The doorbell rang, and Roxy answered it. When Patrick walked in, his face had the same reaction as Rox's. Jax knew he'd done the right thing in renting the tux. He'd wanted to impress Hailey, but at the time he'd started looking at tuxes, he had assumed he would be going as her bodyguard.

Now, he was going as a guest. Still, he couldn't wait to see Hailey's reaction, because that was the one that mattered to him the most. He didn't care what her publicist said or thought of him. The only thing that mattered was what he and Hailey believed. He believed they had a chance together. They just hadn't had enough time to properly spend together.

After tonight, they would.

Patrick sported a smart suit and tie, no tux, and standing next to him, Jax felt a little overdressed. But he was determined to make a great impression at the movie theater and he felt confident that in this attire, he would. "Think she'll be impressed?"

Patrick nodded. "Totally, dude."

He wanted Hailey to see that he could polish up really well— even though she didn't care about such things. It was something he needed to prove, more for himself than anything. He needed to attend that premiere and know that he fit in. That he didn't feel out of place.

"I can just see all the pictures now," gushed Roxy, clasping her hands together in happy pride. "My little bro and Hailey Ross on the cover of a celebrity magazine."

"I don't want that," Jax growled. But if things worked out between him and Hailey, that would be something he'd have to get used to, and for her sake, he would. For her sake, he would do anything she asked.

CHAPTER 34

She had fought hard against getting a limo—the SUV would have sufficed—but Val had insisted on it.

Now it slowly cruised along outside the Knight Movie Theater, instantly bringing to mind the last time she had been here with Jackson.

Huge crowds were gathered outside. A red carpet had been laid. The paparazzi were out in droves. She turned to Val in shock. "I didn't think it would be so big."

"The studio has amped up the event. You're in your hometown, your documentary will air next month. This is great publicity, so work it."

Hailey groaned. She didn't want this, to step out of the limo as if she were someone from a different echelon of society. Technically, given where she now was, this was true, but she didn't feel like that, not anymore. She didn't feel like a stranger returning home for a visit she didn't want.

She felt at home, and part of that was because of the man she desperately scanned the crowd to find. She peered through the tinted windows of the slowly moving limo, heard the cheers, but her mind was on Jackson. She needed to see him. Needed him to soothe her frayed nerves. Needed to look into his eyes and know that this would soon be over, and that she would be with him again.

"You get out first," Val instructed. "Dimitri will be close behind you, and I'll be a few steps behind him. Reed Knight and ..." She peered at her cell phone, "Hya--Hyacinth Fitzsimmons?" she looked at Hailey. "Is that a real person?"

"Yes."

"They'll be standing at the door to greet you with other high-society people. I have no idea how they do things in this place."

The limo finally ground to a halt and the roar from outside amplified.

"Now?" Hailey asked. She hadn't been in front of a crowd like this for a while, the crowd at the mall signing event had been smaller, and that event had been more informal.

This reminded her of Hollywood.

"Yes," Val replied. "Time to get out and work the crowd."

Her nerves jingled, and her heartbeat soared. She was used to huge crowds and loud cheers, to people calling out her name as if they were obsessed by her. But she still needed to take a deep breath and prepare herself.

If Jackson had been here she would have been so much calmer.

Val sucked in a loud breath. "Must you wear that thing around your neck?"

"I must."

"Put on your brightest smile," Val ordered.

"I always do."

The atmosphere between them had chilled. She no longer felt that she could confide in Val, or that this woman had her best interests at heart.

Dimitri appeared and opened her door.

"There's a surprise for you," she heard Val say just as she

stepped out. She was already out of the car and it was too late to stick her head back in to ask her what she meant.

Plastering on a smile, she walked along the red carpet, waving at the crowds on either side. But as she walked around slowly, taking the time to speak to fans in the crowd, signing autographs and letting them take selfies with her, something happened. The love and admiration of the audience melted her hardness. She found herself starting to bask in the warmth of their cheers and obvious delight. With the air charged with electricity, it was impossible not to get caught up in it all.

Conscious of both Dimitri and Val behind her, she scanned the crowd, desperately trying to find Jackson but there was still no sign of him. He was definitely coming. He'd told her. He'd sent her a text message earlier this morning, telling her he couldn't wait to see her.

She couldn't wait to see him.

The paparazzi motioned for her to stand in place, and she posed the way they wanted, holding her glittery clutch in one hand, the other at her neck. She ran her fingers over their initials, as if touching the 'J' and 'H' would magically teleport Jackson to her side.

"Put your hand down," Val hissed under her breath. Hailey smiled, lowered her hand, looked around, wishing and praying that she would soon set eyes on Jackson.

Maybe she had missed him in the crowd. He was here, of that she was sure. Val walked in front of her, leading her towards the entrance to the movie theater. Hailey followed, still stopping to shake hands and meet her adoring fans. Then she heard her name, recognized that voice and turned towards it.

Her breath caught and held in her throat, as if she was too afraid that she might explode with the boatload of happiness that had suddenly burst inside her. Her smile widened, and her eyes welled up, her insides a riot of exhilaration.

There, right at the front, near the doors to the theater, stood Jackson, looking magnificent. He was wearing a tux and he looked jaw-droppingly handsome with his hair swept back, and his eyes shimmering. His hands were casually shoved into his pockets, but he wore that suit so well, that he looked like an A-list celebrity himself. She had become so accustomed to seeing him in his leather jacket and casual clothes that this was a complete shock. A burst of joy exploded inside her. Jackson truly took her breath away.

Val turned to her, "Come on." It wasn't a hiss, she couldn't afford to do that in a crowd like this, but Hailey could afford to ignore her. She beamed at Jackson, and in that moment, when he saw her, time stopped.

It was just her and him, surrounded by noise and a chorus of cheers. She longed to rush towards him, to put her arms around his waist and lose herself in those calming eyes. The string of love and hope connecting them was so strong, she felt a real connection despite them being so far apart.

And then another huge roar erupted from the crowd. Her heartbeat thundered as her confusion grew. Had everyone seen this—her and Jackson? Had their secret suddenly come out?

Val was smiling at her.

Val. *Smiling?*

She was happy for her! Hailey's heart soared. She had been given the green light of Val's approval. If only she could somehow get Jackson to join her. He looked so handsome, her new beau, and she couldn't wait to walk with him on her arm.

"Behind you," Val said, through her smile.

"What?" Hailey turned. A second limo had pulled into view at the far end from where she had just come.

Her insides roiled like a stormy sea, and she felt suddenly unsteady. She wasn't sure what she was seeing. She wasn't sure if this was real. The door opened and Big Rock climbed out, his huge frame making it clear in an instant in case she doubted her eyes.

The crowd erupted in a monstrous roar.

What was he doing here?

She remembered Val's words. Something she had wanted to tell her. The surprise.

"Smile," Val hissed.

Hailey was so stunned, she froze.

Big Rock walked towards her, waving and smiling at the crowd as he did. The contents of her stomach plummeted. Her knees weakened. It all happened in slow motion, Big Rock coming to her, taking her hand, lifting it and kissing the back of it.

Jackson was a few feet away to her right. She could feel his gaze burning into her.

And still Big Rock smiled, and still he kept a hold of her hand, before making her turn around then guiding her towards the entrance to the theater.

She was so numb she only managed to put one foot in front of the other because Big Rock hadn't let go of her hand.

The introductions began, Reed Knight, the man she had so far only heard of, came into view. He introduced her to a group of people. She saw an elderly woman, noticed her bright, garish lipstick as she found herself looking at her.

"Hailey Ross, my dear it is *so* wonderful to have you here..."

Hailey tuned out. She smiled when expected, shook hands, pretended she was happy. And through it all she forced herself to breathe, because her chest had tightened and she struggled for air.

What about Jackson?

Where was he?

She turned her head, but she couldn't see him because there were so many people behind her now, all smartly dressed; the women in full-length gowns and the men in tuxes.

Starling Bay's society.

She caught a glimpse of a couple who looked familiar but it was only when she had walked into the theater and had started walking up the stairs that she realized it had been Dylan and Merry.

Anger collected and simmered in the base of her stomach, mixing with the sadness and shock of what had just taken place.

The studio had gotten its way and was doing all it could to perpetuate this fake romance. They hadn't listened to her at all.

CHAPTER 35

*H*ailey had seen him at last. Jax had been trying to catch her attention, and when their eyes met, his heart almost leapt out of his chest. In that one moment, she was truly happy. He had read her mood, could see that even though she was smiling as she walked along the red carpet, she wasn't truly happy.

He knew this woman as well as he knew himself. That this had happened in such a short space of time only confirmed to him that they were in sync. They were together even when distance tried to keep them apart.

The smile she gave him, only for him, was what he'd been waiting for. She liked him in a tux. It had been worth it, making the effort to dress up, all for her.

For a moment there when she stopped and stared at him directly, he was sure that she was going to come over to him. He didn't want her to. She needed to give the crowd and that agent from hell what they wanted.

He understood that she needed to pacify them, and that once this day was over, they would get their time back.

It was only when another roar from the crowd erupted that he turned to see what everyone was cheering about. But seeing Rick Moretti, the guy Hailey called Big Rock, appear out of nowhere was like a knife to his chest.

What the heck?

"What is this?" Patrick cried. "Who the hell is he?"

He heard Roxy gasp beside him as the actor took Hailey's hand and kissed it.

A cold numbness swept over him. Hailey and Big Rock?

No. It couldn't be.

"Did you know?" Roxy asked him.

"Oh, man." Patrick wailed again.

Hailey never turned and looked at him again. Instead, he had to watch her walk into the movie theater hand in hand with the guy she had claimed had only been her friend. The world and everything in it, suddenly turned dark.

He didn't need this. He couldn't, wouldn't watch any more of this farce. Roxy grabbed his arm as he turned to leave. "Where are you going?"

"Home."

Patrick stood in his way. "Dude, you're all dressed up now. Why waste a good opportunity?"

"Move," he growled. He had no plans to witness this charade.

Roxy tightened her grip on his arm. "Don't go, Jax. Don't. Show her you don't care."

He did care. He was falling for this woman and seeing her with another man had shattered his heart into pieces. "Leave me alone, Rox."

The movie couldn't finish soon enough. She didn't know how she had managed to get through it and not explode. The bile in her throat collected in her stomach. Made her feel queasy and unsettled the whole time.

She hated watching herself on the screen anyway, but premieres were especially difficult. She found them to be generally cringeworthy and she didn't like the way she sounded or looked and was constantly amazed when fans told her they loved her.

But this evening? This evening had been torture. She was desperate to call Jackson. Desperate to find out how he was. Desperate to tell him the truth, but she couldn't go to the restroom or be alone, not without Val and Dimitri following her.

It shouldn't have mattered what they thought or said, but the rage had so clouded her reasoning that she could barely think straight.

She suffered the next few hours after the movie, meeting and mingling with people. Champagne and canapes floated across the air in trays held by smartly dressed servers.

In a place filled with people laughing and talking, with the incessant chatter trickling through the vast lobby, she felt all alone and sad.

Jackson should have been here with her, and they would have wandered around. It would have been such a different experience. She would have been deliriously happy.

Instead, she had cold-shouldered Big Rock. He had disappointed her. They had been friends for so long, but he hadn't had the decency to call and tell her about this stunt.

It was a stunt all right.

Her and Big Rock?

It could never happen. Not in a million years.

She posed with people, trying to fake a smile she didn't feel as the cameras snapped away.

"I'm sorry," Big Rock said to her, grabbing her hand again

and trying to force her away from the crowd into a corner of the room.

"Don't." She snatched her hand away.

"I can explain."

"What you did was inexcusable."

"Why are you so mad?"

He didn't know what she stood to lose, and maybe it was too late, and she had already lost Jackson.

While Dimitri followed her like a shadow, Val kept out of her way.

"Hales!" The familiar voice was like a beacon of light in a storm. "Hales!" This time it was right behind her. She turned to find Claire about to throw her arms around her and give her a hug when Dimitri stepped in to stop them.

"What's wrong?" her friend asked.

"These." Hailey pointed at her earrings and bracelet. "They're worth a few dollars and he's guarding them."

"Your necklace doesn't match," she noted, before asking, "Where's Jackson?"

"Honey, there you are." Claire's husband turned up by her side.

"Hi, Rudy." They exchanged kisses on the cheek. She felt better at seeing people she knew and wanted to be with. They exchanged pleasantries before Claire sent her husband away to fetch a few glasses of champagne for them. "Where's Jackson?" Claire asked again. "Did you see him? He looked so handsome in his tux. *Devastatingly* handsome." She made a swooning motion.

"He's not here. He left when Rick showed up."

"Why?" Her friend looked at her. "Why did he leave, Hales?"

Hailey gave a small shake of her head. Now was not the time or the place to tell Claire about her and Jackson.

"Are you and Rick—"

"No."

Claire's eyebrows lifted almost an inch towards her forehead. "You and Jackson?" she shrieked.

"Shhhhhhhhhhhh." Hailey put her finger to her lips.

"You and Jackson?" her friend cried, this time right inside her ear. Hailey looked at her with doleful eyes.

Yes, her and Jackson. Her boyfriend. The man she wanted to be with. Claire's gaze dropped to the necklace. She examined it, nodding when she separated the two letters. "J and H." Her smile widened. "Oh, Hales!" she gushed. "You lucky thing."

"I don't feel lucky."

"My dear Hailey." Someone grabbed her by the arm just as Claire's husband showed up with the champagne. "Come with me. I want you to meet some people." Hailey wished Hyacinth Fitzsimmons would leave her alone. She gave Claire a mournful look and allowed herself to be whisked away by the woman.

Nothing about today was celebratory, and nothing about it was going the way she had wanted it to.

CHAPTER 36

"Forget about her," said Roxy, handing the server the empty beer bottles as she put new ones on the table.

"Yeah, forget about her, dude," Patrick raised his bottle to his lips and took a big swig. "They're all the same, these Hollywood types."

"And you would know, would you?" Jackson pulled back the pull tab on his can of Pepsi Max.

Patrick slapped him on the back. "Drown your sorrows in beer. You'll soon feel better. That soda isn't going to do jack for you."

"Come on, Jax. Have a beer," Roxy pleaded. "I didn't want to be right about her but—"

"You're not right about her. You don't know her."

"I might have been a little jealous of her once, okay? But now I see her for what she is—a cheat who's with someone else and she didn't tell—"

"Stop, Rox. Just stop." He tilted his head back and took a long drink from the can. He and Hailey hadn't spent much time together at all, not for him to be feeling this torn up about her. But they had shared a connection. For him, these things were rare.

Patrick lifted his bottle and pointed it at him. "I thought she was nice, but it goes to show you how looks can be so deceiving. Someone like that thinks she can play with people's feelings. It's not right."

Jax shook his head. It didn't seem right. None of it. The shock of that moment—of seeing Big Rock take Hailey's hand and kiss it, he thought he'd been watching a scene from a movie play out before him because that moment had been so surreal. Even now he still felt the pain of it, like an open bloody wound.

"Let's play some pool," Patrick suggested again. They had come here to Quinn's after he'd gone home and gotten out of his tux as fast as he could.

He wanted nothing more than to take off on his bike, but Roxy and Patrick had shown up, obviously concerned about him. They had been worried enough that they had insisted on taking him out somewhere, neither one of them leaving his side. This was how they had ended up here, but it still hadn't taken his mind off what had happened. A dark cloud still hung over him and he couldn't see a way out of his misery.

Roxy looked overdressed in her short sparkly dress and Patrick was still in his suit, though he'd removed the tie and jacket long ago. Patrick nudged him. "Let's play another game." They'd been here for hours and while pool was a distraction, he couldn't focus.

"Nah. I'm not in the mood."

They moved from the pool table back to the bar table where every now and then Roxy and Patrick would attempt to make him feel better by telling him it was a good thing he'd found out about Hailey now, and how it was an even better thing that her boyfriend had shown up, because she had clearly looked surprised. Everyone had seen that, though being the consummate performer, she had expertly covered it up and quickly.

He knew, though, because he had come to know her well.

Which was why he couldn't shake that prickly feeling. He picked up his biker jacket.

"Where are you going?" Roxy asked, getting up off her barstool at the same time. She seemed determined not to let him out of her sight.

"I need to get out of here."

Patrick tried to block his path. "Dude, just stay here."

"No."

"Then I'll come with you," Roxy said, grabbing her shiny sparkly bag that matched her dress. She looked so out of place here.

Don't." He motioned for her to stay put. "Don't. I need to be by myself. I need to clear my head."

That's what he needed to do. Clear his head and find out what was really going on.

~

"Why are you getting in the car with me?" Hailey hissed under her breath as Big Rock opened the door to the limo. She glared at Val.

"Smile," Val said, for what felt like the hundredth time that day. She wore that same tight smile which had started to grate on Hailey's nerves from the start. "Get in," Val ordered Big Rock.

The event was over. After the post-movie soiree, she had come outside and spent a long time signing autographs and letting her fans take photos of her. She had done everything that had been asked of her. Nobody realized that inside she was a hot mess. She was dying to get back to her hotel room and start making amends.

She bit down on her teeth as Big Rock climbed into the limo beside her. Her heart was pounding hard and slow. The thought of having to suffer him on the way back made her want to scream, but she was trying to hold it all together.

Jackson didn't want to talk to her. She had tried calling him many times, when she'd been able to sneak a moment alone, but he hadn't answered. And now she as worried about what he would think.

What would he think?

That she had cheated on him?

That she had cheated on Big Rock?

She wanted to explain the whole awful mess and quickly before the situation became irreparable. Because just when she had found someone she could trust, someone who cared for her, everything had slammed to a stop. Again.

"I'm sorry."

Hailey stared out of the window, ignoring Big Rock's apology.

"Are you going back to the hotel?" she asked the driver.

"Yes, ma'am."

She relaxed back in her seat, then opened her clutch and pulled out her cell phone. She tried Jackson again but still it went straight to voicemail.

He'd turned his phone off. She didn't blame him. If he had pulled this kind of stunt, she would never have believed anything he said. But she could explain. She would explain. She would fix this.

"You're going back to the hotel?" she asked Big Rock.

"We're going to switch cars when we're out of sight. Then I'm heading back to LA."

"Why did you come?"

"You know the score, Hailey. I didn't have any say in this."

"You could have warned me."

"Val told me you were okay with it."

"And you believed her?"

"Why are you so angry?" he asked.

She inched her head closer to him, her nostrils flaring. "It wasn't about the romance, was it?"

His forehead puckered and he looked at her, clearly feeling guilty. She nodded, because she knew. She was only one of a handful of people who did; his closest friends knew, and she did because they went back so many years. It was probably only a matter of time before the news broke, but until then, Big Rock was a drop-dead gorgeous guy with an action-man physique and, more to the point, he was the box office's biggest draw right now.

She with her Monica Martins movie character, it wasn't hard to see why the powers that be in Hollywood wanted to spin a story, especially one which might send box office sales through the roof.

Only, this was a story that could never be. Lies aside, she couldn't do this, not to Jackson, not to the man who had a piece of her heart.

She didn't even say goodbye when the limo stopped, and Big Rock got out. Instead she called Jackson again and again, hoping that he would turn his phone back on.

To her relief, the limo started moving again; she had been dreading Val getting in.

Maybe Val was avoiding her, and rightly so.

As soon as the limo reached the hotel. Hailey rushed out. Dimitri appeared by her side from nowhere, as if he had stepped out of the shadows. A small group of fans had gathered outside the hotel lobby.

She was tired and cranky and in no mood to be gracious to fans, so she flashed them the best smile she could, and dove into the open elevator doors with Dimitri hot on her heels.

As soon as she got into her suite, she flung off her jewels, tossing them onto the couch. "There you go. Now you can stop following me around."

She disappeared into her bedroom and shrugged out of her dress and heels. In between getting changed into her comfy clothes, she called Jackson again.

Still no answer.

She flung open her bedroom door, ready to march into the living area, when Val appeared. Hailey slammed her hands on her hips. "That was an underhanded tactic, even for you."

Val's smile faded. "I can explain."

"You could have at least told me."

"I tried to."

"Did you?" Hailey snapped.

It was done. The damage, the ruined event, the chance for her and Jackson to be seen together. She had been touched that he had gone to such efforts to dress up for the event, and now her hopes, like her heart, lay in tatters. "Get. Out."

"What?"

She stood her ground, stared at Val's wide eyes with an unflinching stare. "Get. Out." She had never felt so angry before. Everything she had held in during the day now came pouring out —like molten lava freshly erupted from a liquified earth.

"This was all about ratings and box office sales, Hailey."

"And putting me with Big Rock is going to change that?"

"It was about perception. Giving the fans what they want. It doesn't have to be true. You and Rick don't have to—"

"There is no me and Rick. There never will be."

"Meet me downstairs," Val snapped at Dimitri. She turned to Hailey. "I told you," she said slowly. "Rick Moretti is a big star right now. Possibly bigger than you. It's all about giving fans what they want."

"And what about what I want?" Hailey yelled. "What about the truth?"

"Calm down. What's gotten into you?" Val demanded. "You

were supposed to relax over here in sleepy Starling Bay. I'd say it's made you more uptight—"

"Get out, before I say something I might regret," Hailey warned.

"We're leaving together," Val said. "Pack your things."

"You're leaving. I'm not."

"But I've made an appointment for you to see Dr. Shenkel on Friday."

Hailey cackled. "I am not getting plastic surgery at this age."

"I would advise you to consider it."

"Get out."

"I wasn't the one who issued the directive. I'm not heartless, Hailey."

"You called Jackson a loser."

A flash of knowing flickered across Val's eyes. She took a step back, her mouth falling open. "What is it with you and him? You can't be serious."

"He has my best interests at heart." Something soft and warm blossomed inside her at the thought of him. He was her safe place, her happy place, in a world which was full of fakeness.

"You've changed."

For the better. "Get out before I fire you." Val's eyes popped as if Hailey had grown another head. "Now," snarled Hailey, fighting the urge to march Val to the door herself.

CHAPTER 37

She called Jackson again and still he didn't answer. She couldn't blame him because he probably didn't want anything to do with her after witnessing what he had. After their growing closeness, and their newfound resolve to be together, she had given him reason to doubt her and she was now desperate to see him and put things right.

She pondered on what to do next. She couldn't venture out, because she didn't know where he lived, and she didn't want to get his details from Val. She could go back to the bar, to Quinn's, and maybe find him there. If he was upset, it he might have gone there with his friend.

Once she explained it all, once she fixed it, things could go back to that moment in time that seemed like weeks ago but had only been a few days. She longed for their cozy little bubble of togetherness, just the two of them, with nothing and nobody from the outside world intruding.

But even as she got up from the couch to get ready, she saw that it was getting late. Jackson might be drunk, or still angry, and he might not be ready to see her. Not if he believed that she had lied to him.

Maybe tomorrow she could enlist Claire's help and track him down. The man was hurting, and she was determined to kiss it better.

A knock at the door made her heart skip a beat.

He had come to her.

She rushed to open it, her heart thumping joyously inside her ribcage. It took more than a few seconds for her elation to plummet.

A man she didn't recognize stared back at her. A million thoughts ran riot through her head. "Uh—" she opened her mouth, because he didn't say anything. In the back of her mind, she expected Jackson to spring forth like he had that time Patrick had shown up unexpectedly at her door.

"Hailey," his voice sounded oddly soft, oddly slow. She tried to close the door, but he jammed his foot inside. A burst of fear gave her the shaky strength to try to close the door.

"Don't do this," he said, pushing the door open with alarming ease. She couldn't form a sentence, couldn't think. Fear wrapped its icy fingers around her, turning her blood ice cold, her insides hollow. She stumbled back, watching him walk inside and calmly close the door behind him. "You should go, before my bodyguard finds you," she said in a shaky voice.

"He already left."

The floor seemed to slip out from under her, her unsteady legs threatening to give way. "The other one," she managed to say, staggering back a few more steps until her legs hit the couch, only she couldn't bring herself to sit down. She needed to run. She needed to get away.

"The other one?"

"My boyfriend," she said, forcing her voice to be stronger than she felt.

"He left days ago." The man stood in the center of the room, thankfully not coming any closer.

"You've been watching?"

"I was making sure you were okay."

She blinked. He was calm, *too* calm, and it unsettled her even more as she made a mental note to take in everything about him.

Average height.

Stocky build.

Short buzzcut.

Tattered tracksuit bottoms.

An army jacket.

Piercing blue eyes.

Too bright, too piercing blue.

Her breathing labored. It became a struggle to take in air.

He looked too heavy, too big, too strong, even if she managed to charge past him, she wasn't sure she would be able to open the door and get away.

A shiver rolled up her spine. She rubbed her arms, not feeling cold, but scared. Very scared.

"Sit down, Hailey. You look uncomfortable. Sit down."

She did as he asked.

He pulled over a chair from the main table, turned it around and placed it in front of her then sat with his arms resting on the top of the backrest. He seemed at ease and comfortable.

She tried to think, tried to figure out her escape, but his calm demeanor unsettled her, and her brain fogged over.

"I wondered where you were. You didn't answer my letters."

"Letters?"

He nodded. "I wrote you a letter every day. Sometimes two times a day, but you never answered."

"I... I didn't get them."

"I know, because you were here. I know you didn't leave me. You came here for the premiere."

She swallowed, trying to piece it together. This was the guy who had sent her those letters? This was the reason Val had insisted Jackson be here to guard her, even though she had been insistent that she hadn't needed anyone.

Now she knew, and worse, everyone had left. Jackson, Dimitri, even Val.

She was alone.

"When I found out you were staying here, I kept watch."

"Kept watch?"

"I had to make sure you were okay."

"I am okay. I'm a little tired. It's been a long day."

"I know," he sneered. "I saw you with him."

"With who?"

"I was in the crowd, waving and shouting your name, but you didn't hear me."

"It was busy. There were so many people."

"I came all this way and you didn't even notice me."

"I'm sorry."

"Why did you hold hands with Big Rock?" and before she could answer, "Why are you cheating on me? *Why?*"

She shook her head. "I'm not. I promise you. There's nothing between us."

"You're lying," he snarled. A wave of panic washed over her, and she tried to say something to make him believe her, but her mouth had dried up, as if she'd swallowed sand. Fighting to make her mouth work, she tried to convince him. "I'm … I'm not lying, I swear to you. He's a friend. It was a set up by the studio. I promise you."

"A setup?"

"Yes. They do that. They do that a lot."

His expression seemed to relax. He smiled, and she could hear the blood pounding in her ears.

"You do love me?"

She opened her mouth but struggled to speak. Her voice had gone.

"You do love me," he shouted, his rage exploding.

"Wh-wh-what?"

"You do love me," he said calmly. "Say it."

She swallowed. "I …do …love …"

"SAY IT."

"I do love you."

"I know you do." He grinned at her, and it chilled every bone in her body. "Can I stay here tonight? With you."

"What?" Her voice was barely a whisper.

"Stay here, with you. I've been sleeping outside on the beach, waiting …"

Her chest tightened. "Waiting—fo—fo … for what?"

"For us to be together."

He got into the elevator, memories of the past coming back to haunt him. Memories of the first time he had come to this hotel, to the Blue Velvet Bar, where he had met Hailey and they hadn't gotten off to a good start. The woman was like a chameleon, just when he thought he saw the real her, she would show him another side.

Knowing all that, remembering their long, rollercoaster journey from wary strangers to two people who wanted to be together, he needed to make sense of today.

Something didn't fit and he was determined to get to the bottom of it. He prepared himself for finding a room full of people he would rather not see—Val and that big ugly bodyguard, maybe he could convince Hailey to come to the Blue Velvet Bar with him, and they could find a discreet table so that they could talk. So that he could give her the chance to set things right.

He didn't believe what Patrick and Roxy did. They didn't know Hailey the way he did.

He knocked on her door, and when there was no answer, he knocked again.

Had she left?

Already?

Without calling to tell him?

His phone battery had died long ago when they'd been in the bar, so it was possible that she might have tried to call him.

He knocked again, thought he heard something.

"Hailey?" He rapped his knuckles harder. Put his ear against the door. Heard a man's voice. It could be the bodyguard, or it could be Big Rock.

His hopes crashed to the ground.

Maybe he had it wrong. Maybe he had been so taken in by her beauty that he hadn't taken heed of the warning signs. A woman like that wasn't going to be single.

He knocked again, surprised that she wasn't opening the door. She couldn't face him? Or she was busy?

So be it.

He turned to leave. He had no business being here. He should have listened to Roxy and Patrick.

She was busy with Big Rock. He shook his head as if trying to shake that image out of his head. No wonder she didn't want to open the door.

Yet something pinched in his gut as he walked towards the elevator and pressed the button to descend. She had told him that she wouldn't lie to him. *Ever.* She had been the one to say they needed to tell each other the truth.

Something didn't sit right.

There was no way she would not open the door, to him of all people, even if she and Big Rock were together.

He walked back, pulled out the key card out of his wallet, swiped it and pushed the door open.

What he saw made his gut churn. His worst nightmare. It felt as if someone had punctured his lungs. Hailey looked terrified. In the millisecond it took for him to see her sitting on the couch, her knees pulled up in a defensive position, her arms around her knees as if she were protecting herself, his gaze drifted to the man in front of her.

He wasn't the bodyguard. Nor was he Big Rock.

The man stood up, was about to say something, when Jackson growled. "Who the hell are you?"

In that same moment, Hailey jumped up and rushed to him, falling against his chest, her arms locking around him like a vise. A jolt of awareness shot through him as he sensed her terror, and it unleashed his wrath.

He moved her quickly behind him, protecting her, standing with his chest puffed out, his hands fisted. "Who. The. Hell. Are. *You?*"

"Her boyfriend," the man answered, almost too happily.

"I think he's the one who sent the letters," Hailey whispered. He could feel her face buried against his back, could feel her fingers clinging to his sides. Remembered her fear that day when the drunk had confronted her, knew that this ordeal must have been a million times worse.

"You're mistaken. You see, *I'm* her boyfriend. And you're dead meat."

Confusion on the man's face soon turned to anger as he lunged at Jax, and he, fearful of smashing Hailey against the door leapt forward, blocking the man's onslaught. Jax kicked him between the legs, hard. It was a solid blow, but surprisingly, the man didn't go down right away. He was rock solid, built like a tank and he held up, then came at Jax, throwing him against the wall. He heard Hailey scream, glanced to his side to find her cowering behind a sofa.

By the time he turned back, the man sent a solid hook right to his face. Jax tasted blood. His lip felt numb. Enraged, he landed an almighty punch to the man's chest. He flew back onto the coffee table, landing with a thud so loud, Jax hoped he'd broken something.

But the man still tried to get up. Fueled by blood-red rage, Jax hurled himself at him and they wrestled to the floor. Punches flew. They locked arms, tussling and fighting until Jax straddled him and rained punches down on his face.

In the next few seconds, the hotel's security guards rushed in, probably alerted by the noise.

"Call the police," Hailey screamed.

"Don't take your eyes off him," Jax said, slowly getting up off him as the men took a hold of the culprit's arms. He looked a sorry sight, defenseless and beat, lying on the floor in a bloody mess.

Jax glanced at Hailey cowering in the corner, and rushed to her side, wrapping his arms around her like a safety blanket.

She sobbed against his chest. "I was so scared."

"I've got you," he told her. "I've got you. I won't let anyone lay a finger on you again."

He kissed her head, his eyes still pinned on the man who lay on the floor with two security guards standing over him.

CHAPTER 39

*R*oxy had called him numerous times, worried about him, but in the mayhem and confusion, and with the hotel room full of the hotel's security guards and the police officers, as well as the hotel's manager, Jax hadn't been able to talk to her except to say that all was well and he was with Hailey, and that he would explain later.

"Hailey?" Roxy had screeched.

He had called Val and explained what had happened, because Hailey was still too shaken up to talk. He could only imagine. The look on her face as he had walked in was one he would never forget. Just like he would never have forgiven himself if anything had happened to her.

When Val asked to speak to Hailey, she declined, and it was only when Val threatened to return to Starling Bay with Dimitri in tow that Hailey grabbed the phone off him.

"*Don't* come back. And you had better put out a press release stating that Big Rock and I are nothing but friends. If you tell the truth, you won't have to put a spin on it." She handed the phone back to him and he promptly hung up.

"A spin on it?" he asked, holding her against his chest. The hotel suite was empty now, and it was way past midnight with just the two of them cuddled up on the couch. "What spin?" He slid his fingers between Hailey's silky hair, inhaled the scent of fresh apples and the outdoors—something that would always remind him of her.

"About Big Rock and me."

He swallowed, tried to prepare himself for news which would puncture the hope that had started to mushroom inside him.

"I'm not with Big Rock," she told him. "I never have been."

"Then what was he doing here?"

"Helping the press with their lies."

He frowned, not understanding, but he also didn't want to pressure her too much, not after what she had been through. But he needed to know about them. About him and whether there was any chance for anything. "What about us, now?"

She looked up at him, her slim brows revealing her confusion. "Now I'm with you. Are you with me?"

Boom, boom, boom. Tiny fireworks went off in his chest. He could not have hoped for more uplifting words. They spoke of a future that he had never envisioned for himself. "Of course I'm with you."

"Sure?"

He nodded. "I've been twisted up in knots ever since I saw you and him, Big Rock, kissing your hand, holding hands. I couldn't believe what I was seeing."

She lifted up on her knees and kissed him on the lips. "I saw your face. I saw you in your tux. You looked so handsome, Jackson. I wanted you to be with me, on the red carpet walk. I wanted to walk into that movie theater with you and no one else."

"Then why did he come?"

"It's a game. Strategizing. Publicity. He's a big hit, and I'm on my way down—"

"No, you're not. Don't let anyone convince you that you are."

"Ratings don't lie. Box office sales don't lie."

"I've watched all your movies."

"All of them?"

"All of them. I've been living in a Hailey-bubble for weeks, seeing you and being with you during the day and then watching your movies back in my room."

She giggled. "You overdosed on me."

"I can never get enough of you." It was a confession.

"That makes two of us," she said. His gaze was pinned on her lips, luscious and full, and he couldn't resist the urge to fall into another sweet kiss.

"I was so lucky that you came. Why did you come?" she asked.

"To talk to you."

"Your phone was on voicemail the whole time. I kept calling you, needing to explain."

"My phone battery died, and I couldn't charge it up. We went to Quinn's, me, Roxy and Patrick."

Hailey made a face when he mentioned Roxy. "Your sister doesn't like me."

"My sister doesn't know you."

"I don't know her, but I didn't hate her on sight," she countered.

"True. Roxy isn't so bad once you get to know her. She's having a hard time with her diner. Things aren't going so great and it sucks because she works so hard."

"What does that have to do with me?"

"Nothing. Nothing at all. I hope I've made her see that."

"Why would you make her see that?"

"Because she means a lot to me, and you mean the world to me. It would be nice for the two of you to get along."

Hailey opened her mouth to protest.

"I know. I know you've done nothing to her. It's on her, and in time, she'll come and apologize to you for not giving you a chance."

"I don't need her to apologize to me. I just need her to be nice."

"I know."

It depended on what was going to happen between them. If he and Hailey went their separate ways soon after her stay here ended, then Rox and Hailey would never really meet much and it wouldn't matter.

"You went to Quinn's," she prompted.

"They wanted me to stay at the bar with them, but I needed to come here. I had to hear what you had to say about Big Rock, and him showing up like that. I needed to know why you hadn't told me about him."

"Because there was no 'him' to tell you about. Big Rock isn't going to pull a stunt like that again."

"Does he have feelings for you?"

She laughed, then clamped her lips together as if she was stopping herself from saying something.

"What?"

"I'm going to break my code of honor, but only because you mean the world to me, and I want you to know that Big Rock is nothing to worry about."

"Break your code of honor?" What was she talking about? He didn't know whether to be anxious, or to prepare for a sense of relief.

"Rick's gay. I've known for years."

Gay? He'd never seen that coming. He'd had an idea that something was off, that something didn't fit right. He couldn't believe that Hailey would do something like that to him. He *knew* her, and this was why—despite what Roxy and Patrick said—that he couldn't believe it.

There had to have been a reason for Big Rock's sudden

appearance. Jax had imagined the worst, thinking that the guy had had a crush on Hailey, that maybe there had been a flash of attraction between them in the past, and that this had been his way of wanting to show her that he was interested, by turning up at a big event.

It would have been hard, but he could have lived with that, as devastating as it would have been, but what Hailey was telling him now was the best thing he could have hoped for.

She didn't feel anything romantic for the man, and Big Rock wasn't interested in women, so Jackson would never have to worry about him.

"It's still a secret," she said quickly, "I have no idea how he's managed to keep it quiet in a place like LA, but he has." She frowned. "At least I think he has."

"Maybe the rumors have started to fly," he suggested. "And what better way to slay those rumors than by having him be seen with Hollywood's sexiest and most beautiful star?"

"Stop it," she cried, swatting him playfully.

"But you are." He entwined his hand in hers, rubbed his thumb over her soft skin, and felt at peace. He could see himself sitting with Hailey, spending countless evenings like this.

"I want to sit on this couch with you and watch TV and eat popcorn all night long," she said, beginning to sound more like the woman he had started to get to know before that useless piece of filth had walked into her hotel room and scared her half to death.

"We can do that." He wasn't going anywhere. She lifted her head up and stared into his eyes, her guard was down, and his was coming down by the minute. He would give his life for her. Keep her safe, protect her for always. "We can do it the day after that, and the day after that, and the day after that," he promised, before leaning down and planting a soft kiss on her lips.

Exhilaration rushed through his veins, an excitement the likes of which he had never felt before. Hailey erased all the kisses and imprints of his past girlfriends. She had made him hers, and he basked in the beautiful hope of this promise.

"You saved my life, Jackson."

He put his arms around her, hugging her to his chest, vowing never to put her in danger again. It didn't matter that the other bodyguard had deserted her, he shouldn't have left her alone, not after what Val had told him. In fact, he was shocked that Val had left her, even if Hailey was the one who had told her to go. Val should have known better, and so should he have.

But he had come in time, and he had come through. She was safe now, and he would keep her safe for as long as she needed him.

This was as real as it got; Hailey and him, no gimmick, no publicity stunt, no fake romance.

CHAPTER 40

*R*oxy had invited them over to his place. Jackson said his sister wanted to make up for how she had been with Hailey before. They had embraced upon meeting one another, and then made lots of civil and polite conversation before Hailey slipped out into the hallway to take the call from Val.

She had no desire to talk to this woman, but she also didn't want the burden of not knowing why she had called hanging over her head during a dinner which she wasn't sure would be completely easy.

"When are you coming back?" Val wanted to know.

"I don't know. I haven't thought about it." She was enjoying life. Enjoying every moment of every day.

"You can't stay there forever. Think of your career, Hailey."

"Leave that thinking to me."

"Do you know what you're doing?"

"I know perfectly well what I'm doing. I've been doing this for more years than you have. *I* decide how my career goes. Not you. I decide what roles I want. Not you, not the studio. Oh, and I'm taking the summer off."

"But you have auditions!"

"I don't like any of the scripts you've sent me."

"You signed up to complete three more movies in the Monica Martins franchise."

"I'll honor that, but I want to branch out so in the future, only send me scripts for thought-provoking serious roles. I don't want to be remembered as a pin-up." She hung up. Keeping her calls with Val short was a good thing.

"Everything okay?" Jackson asked, his voice sexy and soothing at the same time. She barely had time to turn around when he slid his arms around her from behind.

"It was Val."

He groaned. "Can't that woman ever leave us alone?"

Hailey turned her cell phone off in front of him. "Now she will." She tried to get out of his embrace, not wanting Roxy to think she was being rude. But Jackson had other ideas. He spun her around so that she was facing him, and then slid his hands around her back. Her body reacted and she instinctively slid her arms around his neck as their lips met. Kissing him was like flying through the sky; he made her feel weightless, and free, and giddy all at once.

"Ahem." They broke apart, and she felt embarrassed that Roxy had caught them kissing in the hallway as if they'd sneaked out just for this.

"I was … I was … I had to take a phone call," she explained to his sister. This new occurrence of Roxy inviting them over for dinner was an olive branch, one that she was determined to accept with both hands.

Jackson had already told her that Roxy meant a lot to him, and Hailey was determined to have a good relationship with her, not just for Jackson's sake, but because she recognized in Roxy some of her own determined stubbornness to make good.

"How long have you been standing there?" Jackson asked, not allowing her to break out of his embrace easily.

"Long enough to see that you two are so good together." Roxy took a tiny step closer and looked at her. "I said some unpleasant things to Jax about you not being right for him, but I want you to know that I was only protecting him. I didn't want him to get hurt, and I thought with you that might happen. I was wrong and I'm sorry. You make him happy. I don't think I've ever seen my little bro look happier."

The directness of the apology touched a nerve. Until now, neither of them had said anything about the earlier frostiness.

She smiled at Roxy. "Thank you for saying that. It means a lot to me. Let's put this behind us."

Roxy nodded, and pulled at the dishrag in her hand. "Dinner is being served. Shall we eat?"

Dinner smelled divine. Hailey was fed up with having room service and takeout food—even if it was from Fellini's. Nothing beat home-cooked food, and the aroma of steak and potatoes wafting over made her salivate. Her salad and water days were long gone. Or maybe until she needed to get back on the set of her next movie.

For now, it was carbs, carbs and more carbs all the way.

These lazy days with Jackson, shooting pool at Quinn's, her and Jackson having dinner with Claire and Rudy at their home, and then all of them going to dinner at Fellini's, these were real-life experiences. They meant something. They were also the building blocks to the happier future she had never imagined for herself.

Jackson had given her a chance.

Normal life.

Incredible love.

It was too soon to think about the future, but they had discussed a few things, the main one being that she and Jackson would never be apart. He would be her security detail for now, and live in LA when she needed to be there, and the rest of the time they would spend in Starling Bay.

This glittering little town with its charming little places, and its people, with their intricately woven lives, these held a place in her heart, all the more so because of the man she loved.

Returning to her hometown, she felt as if she had come full circle.

"Do you want to go in?" Jackson asked as they took off their helmets. They had just parked in the Clearwater parking lot.

She shook her head. She had only glanced at the astrology shop but she had no intention of going in. She didn't need a mystic to tell her what she already knew, that Jackson was a rare thing, the type of man she had never met but had always dreamed of, someone strong and good and sexy, yet with a vulnerability that made her want to protect him just as much as he protected her.

"We should go into the gift shop, though, to see the owners. They were at the movie premiere and I wasn't in such a good mood back then."

That day was still vivid in her mind, as was what had happened later with the stalker who had calmly walked into her hotel suite. She shivered and pushed the thought away, letting Jackson take her hand, the way he always did. She squeezed it, needing the reassurance and strength, the reminder that she had had a lucky escape.

"Do you want to go in now?" He lifted up the small picnic

basket Roxy had prepared for them. They had only passed through the diner, but she hadn't known that Jackson had planned a day in the woods, or that Roxy had put together a picnic basket filled with heaps of delicious little nibbles.

"I was thinking that we could go in and see how Merry is." They should have done it sooner but the last few weeks had been a blur. "Reed's girlfriend said she was being sick in the toilet at the premiere."

"She was?"

Hailey nodded. She was starting to strike up friendships with a few people she and Jackson had met during their walks around the town and on the beach. There were also people she was keen to avoid.

Like the busybody Hyacinth Fitzsimmons. The woman had been trying to convince Hailey to take charge of the Christmas pageant this year and Hailey had so far given her a firm no, though Hyacinth didn't seem to be the type of woman who would take no for an answer.

If she had to, she would whisk Jackson away to New York for a surprise Christmas break, or to her Santa Monica home. Anything to get out of the pageant.

"Can we see her on the way back?" Jackson suggested. "I don't want that great big dog sniffing around Roxy's picnic basket."

"Agreed. We shouldn't waste this yummy food."

They set off towards the woods, the sunshine falling through the leaves and branches of the trees warmed her and put a golden glow upon the day which was already bright and beautiful.

It had only been a month since the premiere, but she had taken rein of the direction of her life, instead of leaving it to her agent and the whims of Hollywood. Slowly, things were starting to fall into place in a way that they weren't quite falling into place for her career-wise, but she was in no hurry. She had proved herself, and she was eager to get off the hamster wheel of success and all the worry that came with being at the top of her game.

Next week she and Jackson would fly to LA. She hadn't returned yet, and now seemed as good a time as any given that there were many things to tie up there. It would be a good time for Jackson to get a glimpse of her life in Hollywood.

Living in a hotel suite here wasn't ideal, and last week a chance meeting with someone Jackson knew, a realtor by the name of Rourke, had given her the idea of finding a more permanent place to live here. They would see about hunting for a home in Glassmere.

It was a grand start, but she felt as if it was the start of a more fulfilling life. Perhaps a life with children, a family, a life that was possible because of Jackson.

"That was nice of Roxy," she said, pondering over the many things Roxy had done for them. Little things, like putting this picnic basket together for them; meaningful things that money could not buy.

"It's nice that the two of you are getting along."

"I wish I could do something for her."

Now that they were spending more time together and had been to Roxy's Diner a few times, she had seen with her own eyes how hard Roxy worked.

"You don't need to do anything," Jackson said.

"For her business."

"She'll be fine. Things will turn around."

"But she works all the time." Hailey stopped walking as the perfect solution flashed through her head. "I know just the thing that can help her. I know just the man."

Jackson frowned. "Rox isn't looking for a man."

"That's not what I mean. This man can *help* her."

"How?"

"Have you watched that TV show, the one with Mason

Brandt, the celebrity chef who goes in and fixes problems that restauranteurs are having?"

Jackson laughed. "Who?"

"Mason Brandt. You'll know if you saw him. He's a friend of mine, and he's got a TV show where he helps turn failing restaurants around."

Jackson shook his head and they continued walking. "Rox would never agree to anyone telling her how to run her kitchen, least of all a celebrity, and least of all a man. That's just asking for trouble, babe. It won't work."

"But you can see she's struggling and unhappy. Don't you want to help her?"

Jackson groaned. "Trust me, a celebrity chef isn't going to be any help. Not to Rox. Also, I don't think she would consider her restaurant as 'failing'."

"It doesn't have to be badly failing. The diner isn't failing, it's just not scaling the way she wants. Mason can help things around so that profits are higher. It's exactly what Roxy needs."

Jackson winced. "My sister doesn't take help easily from people. You've met her. You know what she's like."

Hailey did know what Roxy was like, but she also knew that his sister couldn't continue working so hard without anything changing. She was certain that this man could help her. "I'll give him a call when we get back."

"We could be a while." Jackson gave her one of those knowing looks. "We have a blanket, and we have food, and we have these...these...trees and stuff."

She giggled. "Trees and stuff." She squeezed his hand again, content and grateful for this man, and this day. "You love being out here."

"Only 'cause I love being with you." He threw his arm around her shoulder.

LA with its fast life and Ferraris, and the glamor and glitz of

Hollywood, dimmed and disappeared when she was with Jackson. Starling Bay and all the things she loved about it were center stage in her mind.

Days like today were more precious than movie accolades and mansions. Butterflies swarmed inside her stomach at the thought of the future and the promise that it held.

Thank you for reading **Guarded Hearts!**

I hope you enjoyed Hailey and Jax's story.

You can still read more about them in the next book, **Table for Two**. This is Roxy's story and you can read a first chapter excerpt at the end of this book.

If this is the first Starling Bay book you've read, you might want to start with the first book, **Winter's Kiss.**

If you'd like to be notified of new book releases and more, please subscribe to my newsletter here:

http://www.siennacarr.com/newsletter

Thank you,

Sienna

ACKNOWLEDGMENTS

I would like to thank my amazing group of proofreaders who check my manuscript for errors, typos and inconsistencies.

I am eternally grateful for their help and support:

Marcia Chamberlain
Nancy Dormanski
Dena Pugh
Carole Tunstall

I would also like to thank Tatiana Vila of Vila Design for creating this awesome cover.

ABOUT THE AUTHOR

Sienna Carr is a pen name for an author who has been writing romance since 2013. She lives in the UK with her husband, three children, and a parrot.

Connect with Me

I love hearing from you – so please don't be shy!
You can email me at: sienna@siennacarr.com